W. K Weare

Songs of the Western Shore

W. K Weare

Songs of the Western Shore

ISBN/EAN: 9783337008987

Printed in Europe, USA, Canada, Australia, Japan

Cover: Foto ©Andreas Hilbeck / pixelio.de

More available books at **www.hansebooks.com**

OF THE

WESTERN SHORE.

BY

W. K. WEARE

OF NEVADA.

SAN FRANCISCO:
BACON & COMPANY, PRINTERS.
1879.

TO THE

PIONEERS OF THE WESTERN COAST

THIS VOLUME

IS RESPECTFULLY DEDICATED

BY A

BROTHER PIONEER.

PREFACE.

In submitting this little effort to the appreciation of the people of the Pacific Coast in general, and the Pioneers of the Western Shore in particular, I might say that I was urged to such action by the solicitation of my innumerable friends. But I forbear, fearing the inevitable "Too thin"; and will say that the fact set forth in "The Miner's Surprise," in the sentence "I represent the prodigals who came in Forty-nine," has more to do with my action; and that necessity, as much as inclination, was the motive power. I have endeavored to set forth my ideas in simple style, without the aid of impracticable meters or inapplicable metaphors. Should the morosely critical say that both the matter and manner are foreign to the meaning of the title, I shall only say that I had the ambition, whether laudable or not, to endeavor to draw attention to some existing abuses or misconceptions which I conceived to be hindrances to the advancement of our peculiar polity, and the aims of refined civilization, which

I could not effect under a less alluring title, more especially for the young. If I shall disabuse the minds of a class among the community of a mistake under which they labor, and prove that the Pioneers are not the old " stiffs " and fossils they are supposed to be ; that they are not buried in the ruins of Forty-nine so deep as to be oblivious to the exigencies and necessities of the living present, I shall have accomplished all I anticipated and more.

W. K. W.

CARSON CITY. October, 1879.

CONTENTS.

Songs of the Western Shore.

ODE TO THE PIONEERS.

Magician! Memory! break the spell of intervening time
While we rehearse the deeds of old wrought by a faith
    sublime,
Since when on the Sierra's crest a Pioneer first trod,
When all was wild as when it sprang from chaos or from
    God—
        To light, and life, and action then!
        Bring forth upon the scene the men
            Whom memory still endears.
        The brave, the bold, the tried and true!
        Who made this land a home for you—
            The grand old Pioneers!
        Who paved the way for empire here,
        Who never knew a doubt or fear,
        Who led proud Progress year by year—
            Hail! and a thousand cheers!
    *   *   *   *   *   *
For some toiled o'er the desert waste, while through the
    night in dreams

They heard the savage war-whoop wild, or wife and children's screams;

Or saw by day some victim's scalp reeking with crimson
gore—

What tongue can tell the suff'ring passed to reach the
Golden Shore?

Beneath the burning sun by day, the gleaming stars by
night,

Onward they toiled across the pale dull, desolated blight,

Until from the Sierra's crest they saw the promised land

Whose mountain torrents dashed along o'er beds of
golden sand.

Their feet trod Colorado's plains and Arizona's soil,

Despite of danger, hunger, thirst, or wild Apache broil.

The highest mountain had for them no danger to affright,

They climbed without a sign of tire each regal crest of
white.

Nor hireling slaves were ever they, but free as mountain
air.

They sought the treasure in the wild, the wild beast's life
to share,

Till each lone crag, and dark ravine, and cañon's murky
cave,

Has been since first the land they trod some Pioneer's
lone grave.

The half they did there's none can know—it never can
be told:

The trail is paved, o'er which they passed, with silver and
with gold.

They planned the City of the Bay, which proudly may
aspire

To grandeur far transcending that of old imperial Tyre;

They formed its types along the way to Davidson's high
crest,

Where sits Virginia, silver-robed, the wonder of the
West;

They brought the rivers to the plains unblessed by summer showers;

They made the wilderness to bloom with vines and orange
bowers.

No grander monument than theirs on earth can ever be—

Its apex, the Sierra's crest; its base, Magellan's Sea.

* * * * * *

Now, every day we hear of some whose earthly bonds
are riven,

Whose hands their last deep shaft have sunk, their last
lone tunnel driven.

Let's hope that in the Fatherland they're called on to
explore

Are treasures richer, brighter, far than gold or silver ore.

For, while the glorious West shall live the pride of
future years,

Thousands of happy homes must bless the grand old
Pioneers.

SONG OF THE "BULLION."

Where the snowy crests of the mountains towered
  O'er an aspect stern and wild,
Where no harvests gleamed in the autumn sun,
  Or the flowers of the garden smiled,
For ages I lay in my gloomy shroud,
  Unblessed by the Day-God's beam,
Ere the igneous floods of the earth well'd forth
  In the lava's fearful stream.

I was there ere the Shepherd Kings of old
  Worshipped the rainbow fair,
And thought that it rose from the shades of death,
  And was born from the breath of prayer;
That its aureole stripes, with their golden light,
  Reached over the wide earth's rim,
To carry the prayers of the culprits up
  To the Throne and the cherubim.

I was there ere the towers of the Nile were seen,
  Or a pyramid raised its head,
Or Egyptian graves in the solid rock
  Were filled with the mighty dead.
Ere the Orient nations waxed and waned
  In the ages long since gone,
Or the Eastern World bowed down before
  The giants of Macedon.

I was here in the wilds of our wondrous West
  Ere its empires rose and fell;
But none invaded my lone retreat,
  Or dared in these woods to dwell.
Yes, cycles of ages before the time
  When was peopled the verdured earth,
And the age when its burning cauldron cooled,
  Was the date of my fiery birth.

But *now!* I am Lord of the land and sea—
  All bow to my mighty power,
And the loftiest head bends meekly low
  For a tithe of my princely dower.
I bring to my arms from distant lands
  The fruits of the teeming earth,

From my path in despair flies the vulture Want,
    While hope in the heart finds birth.

Do you ask why so long in my shroud of gloom
    I lay in my hidden lair?
Why I came not forth to the glorious light,
    A boon to a world more fair?
Go! ask of the Mighty One who rules
    The universe supreme:
I abode His time in the darksome caves,
    Unblessed by the Day-God's beam—

To come forth at the time when tyrants mocked,
    And traitor hands were raised,
When the long-pent fires of a smouldering hate
    O'er the walls of Sumpter blazed.
Then I came, a boon to the gallant ranks
    Of the millions brave and true,
Who were sworn to the stars of the grand old flag
    Bequeathed by the patriot few.

Do you ask who am I who in haughty pride
    Bend the earth to my stubborn will?
At whose frown the fiery passions rise,
    At whose smile the fiends are still?

Ye have known my name, ye have owned my power!
From the time of your birth 't was told.
I am "Bullion," seen in the silver's sheen
And the gleam of the radiant gold.

The utilization of the silver from the Comstock was nearly coeval with the attack on Sumpter, and from that time a continuous stream of bullion flowed into the treasuries of the Sanitary and Christian Commissions. Had it not been for the discovery of gold, and the millions thrown into the lap of the nation, 't is doubtful whether our credit would have carried us through the war. And had the Western Slope been in sympathy with the South and the stream of bullion gone there, the result would have been entirely different. The Union could not have been preserved.

SONG OF THE BATTERY.

Turn the torrent wild from its rocky bed,
   Chain the princely power of steam.
That my arms may be nerved by their giant strength
   Let me hear the whistle scream.
For my revel is not on the field of strife,
   I herald no deadly fight
Where the victor Death is the power that reigns,
   And Might claims the meed of Right.

No! my revel is not on the field of blood,
   Like the " batteries " known of yore;
My harvest is not in the crimson flood—
   It is gleaned from the shining ore.
And as death follows fast on my namesake's track,
   So life follows fast on mine,
For I bring to the light and I scatter and spread
   The wealth of the darksome mine.

Whole ages had passed, and the busy world
  ' Mid these scenes saw no prospect fair;
Its vales were the wandering Indian's home,
  Its mountains the wild beast's lair.
I came! and the sound of my iron tramp
  Is now heard where a sound can stray,
While the toilers come from Atlantic's shores,
  And the realm of the old Cathay.

They shall come our mountain slopes to gird,
  And our river beds to span,
Till my tramp shall be heard in a thousand vales
  Even now unknown to man—
Till iron bands shall the shores unite
  Of the North with the Tropic Sea,
And desert plains show the springing germs
  Of an Empire yet to be.

Yes! my tramp shall be heard in the northern land.
  O'er the shriek of the Borean breeze;
' T will be heard by the child of the southern clime,
  Near the shores of the Tropic Seas.
In cradle lands of our ancient race
  Is the spell of my power confessed;

They are lured to the scene of my conquests now,
  In the wilds of the wondrous West.

Oh! they sang of the wealth of the Orient clime
  On the far-famed Indian shore;
Of the treasure Spain in her hour of pride
  From the land of the Aztec bore;
Of diamonds bright, from Brazilian sands—
  But the fruit of my tireless tramp
Is to such, as the Pole-Star's steady gleam
  To the glare of Aladdin's lamp.

And they sang, in the ages long since passed,
  Of the fabled Age of Gold;
But it only lived in the realm of song
  Till I came to the wealth unfold
Long locked in the mountain's rocky caves,
  Unknown to the ancient sage;
I am king of the real Age of Gold,
  I am king of the Mineral Age.

Then turn from its bed the river's force,
  Chain the princely power of steam,
That my arms may be nerved by their giant strength;

Let me hear the whistle scream.
For I am the king of the mountain land,
   With my clangor, and crash, and shock,
As with tireless tramp I tear from its home
   The wealth in the stubborn rock.

VIRGINIA CITY, 1866.

CARRIE:

THE TRAGEDY OF LAKE TAHOE.

'T was summer! and only the last fading trace
   Of the winter's snow-mantle was seen;
And the rivulets, freed from the Storm King's embrace,
   Rippled on amid islets of green.
When our path lay along the Sierra's steep side,
   Near the shore of its beautiful lake,
When our voices turned silent, their echoes had died,
   And I thus strove the stillness to break.

"Come, cheer up!" I said; "does some Sibyl, whose haunt
   Is this fastness, cast o'er you her spell?
In what sylvan retreat from some battle with want
   Does she live—the enchantress? Come, tell!
Come, tell me the legend." The mountain peaks rise,
   Like sentinels watching above;
In the lake's placid bosom lie mirrored the skies,
   While each zephyr seems laden with love.

24

Then he spake, as his glance seemed to wander away
   To some land past my vision—unknown :
From the mountain cliff there, overlooking the Bay,
   His heart-sorrow he slowly made known.
'T was a fact; no wild dream of the poet his tale,
   Who by fancy has peopled each cave ;
Who sees in each grotto some recluse, lone, pale,
Past the malice or envy of earth to assail,
   Companioned by gloom or the grave.

" Well, 't is nearing a year, since the bright summer day
   Seemed to her, the most fair 'midst the fair,
As bright as Aurora in spring-time and May,
   Ere mankind knew of sorrow and care,
When a young merry band left the lake-shore below
   To gaze on these wonders around;
Brave youths and fair maidens, as pure as the snow,
   With which yonder tall mountain is crowned.

" But like her who the prize at Mount Ida once won,
   There was one still more fair 'midst the fair,
One whose eyes of sweet blue caused the heartless to shun
   Their glance for the realm of despair;
As lithe as a Naiad, with step light as floss,
   Or the gossamer floating in dew;

2

None saw but to love her, none can know my loss;
  To each duty of life ever true.

" Do you see? over *there!* in that cleft in the rock,
  That flower, on the precipice, *there?*
Just heaven, you see it! I still feel the shock,
  And remember my impotent prayer.
She sprang, with the dash of a mountain gazelle,
  To the edge of the cañon's steep side—
She grasped it! one moment! oh God, must I tell?
  Yes, down! down! in her beauty and pride,
To the foot of the chasm, all mangled, she fell,
  There my daughter, my all on earth died!

" Sometimes, when the winter blast howls down the steep,
  And the Storm King his tempest-song sings,
I awake. Was it fancy? A phantom of sleep?
  Or the voice of my darling that brings
Me still nearer her home-land? Yes, darling, I know
  By the shores of the Idyllic Sea,
In the summer's soft calm, or when winter winds blow,
  I still hold sweet communion with thee.

"And all else is forgotten. The laughter and shout
  Wake no chord to respond in my ear;

There's a Spirit Land, friends, past this region of doubt,
  Where the summer skies always are clear;
Where no winter storms rage, and where sorrow's un-
  known,
  And the trustful are never beguiled;
From that Land there's a call, and the music's my own;
  'T is the voice of my darling, my child!"

NOTE.—Near or in the hamlet of Glen Brook, on the eastern shore of Lake Tahoe, "the Gem of the Sierras," there arises an abrupt rocky prominence. Seen from some positions the rock outlines a human profile, and is thought to look like the face of Shakespeare; hence 't is called "Shakespeare's Rock." Near the end of the summer of 1877, a band or company of young people climbed the rock, which is quite a common feat with tourists. Among them was Miss Carrie E. Rice, a young lady well known, and beloved by all. In springing to an isolated cleft or step she fell, and was mangled, crushed to death. The verses are a delineation of the circumstance. as told the writer on the spot.— W. K. W.

EL ARBOL DEL MADRONA.

On the wild mountain-side, where the forest trees, blend-
  ing,
Enshroud the surroundings in shadow and gloom,
And the tall, somber fir, in stern grandeur ascending,
  Imparts to the scene the repose of the tomb;
Where the wild bird or beast, when by danger af-
  frighted,
  Turns from its destroyer in terror to flee—
There, in evergreen splendor, the eye meets, delighted,
  The beauteous Madrona, the "Strawberry Tree."

Where the bleak, rocky cliffs overhang the deep gorges,
  Whose crash would the bravest with terror appall;
Whose storm-riven fragments the element forges
  To bowlders, rough-hewn by the force of their fall;
Where the stormy wind moans, and the tempest, career-
  ing,
  Strikes notes of weird music in Nature's wild key—

There, the stern desolation enlivening and cheering,
    Stands the beauteous Madrona, the " Strawberry Tree."

The Tropics may boast of their rich, verdant splendor,
    Their groves, blossom-laden, soft breathing of balm;
Boast of wild, tangled vines, which do beauty engender
    Round the stately magnolia or green-crested palm;
But *here*, where around all is darksome and dreary,
    And the eye seeks in vain some oasis to see,
Thy gorgeous resplendence is spread for the weary,
    Thou beauteous Madrona, the " Strawberry Tree."

Perennial, effulgent, with verdure unfading,
    In the autumn, who seeks may with transport behold
Thy leaves and thy fruit, some lone grotto enshading,
    Where the emerald blends with the hue of the gold.
Unique and fantastic, thy arms gently waving,
    Show beauty transcending all mortals may see,
The homage of lovers of nature enslaving,
    Thou beauteous Madrona, the " Strawberry Tree."

The birds midst thy branches, their melody pouring,
    Seem delighted to find in the dim sylvan scene
Some object to call forth fresh notes of adoring,

While through the dense foliage bright gleams inter-
    vene.
The brook bubbles onward, fulfilling Thy orders,
    And murmurs devotion, kind Heaven, to Thee,
Who hath placed on Earth's rocky and storm-riven bor-
    ders
    The beauteous Madrona, the "Strawberry Tree."

The Madrona, or Strawberry Laurel, is a native of California, and under favorable circumstances attains a large size. Its bark is a buff, some shades darker than the Manzanita, or "Little Apple," and of the same family. During the autumn of 1854, while hunting on the Coast Range of mountains, I came suddenly upon four specimens of gigantic size. They were growing near a mountain brook, and are always an indication of water. These were in full fruitage. The clusters were as large as the largest of the grape, each individual berry being a fac-simile of the strawberry, of a rich golden color. The leaves are long and pendent, and of a glossy, enameled green. The blending of the colors presented a picture of rare beauty. Hundreds of birds were feasting among the branches. "Como se llama aquel arbol?" I asked of my Mexican friend, ("How do you name that tree?" being literal English). "Es el Madrona, señor," ('T is the Strawberry Tree, sir,") was the answer. "Es la fruta buena para comer?" ("Is the fruit good to eat?") I asked. "Pienso es veneno," ("I think 't is poison") was the answer. "Mira! mira! señor! los pajaros se comen! El Señor ha enseñado los pajaros mas que los hombres" ("Look! look! the Lord has shown the birds more than man") I answered, in my American Spanish; and then, drawing my note-book. I wrote, "El Arbol del Madrona."

"LA FLOR DEL MARIPOSA,"

Or "THE BUTTERFLY FLOWER."

Hie away! hie away from the haunts of men,
  To the mountains come with me,
When the burning beams of the summer sun
  Wilt a leaf on the greenest tree.
If a sense of beauty you claim to own,
  If that be a part of your dower,
You will thrill with delight when first you see
  The beautiful " Butterfly Flower."

For it lives not by the rivulet's side,
  Nor deep in the grassy glade ;
But it chooses the parched, unsheltered plain,
  Afar from the cooling shade.
It is a child of the genial sun,
  'T is not a child of the shower,

And it gathers its life from the Day-God's beams,
   The beautiful " Butterfly Flower."

It comes not forth in the flush of spring,
   When the earth is clothed in green ;
'T is not till the sun pours his fiercer rays
   That its beauteous face is seen.
The lava soil, which it seems to love,
   Bestows no fragrant power ;
But no art can copy the matchless tint
   Of the beautiful " Butterfly Flower."

It closes its leaves at the night's approach,
   When its patron sinks to rest,
Enfolding with all a mother's care
   The petals within its breast.
And not till the sun sheds forth his ray,
   Long past the rising hour,
Do its leaves expand to the light of day,
   The beautiful " Butterfly Flower."

A child of the mountain, a child of the sun,
   And a child of the barren soil,
It seems to breathe a lesson of love
   To the children of want and toil.

'T is cultured not in a gay parterre,
Nor the foundling of pride or power,
But 't is sent to adorn the dreary wild,
The beautiful " Butterfly Flower."

And ye who repine at your gloomy lot
In this world of want and care,
Should know that wherever your steps may trend
There is something bright and fair ;
That nature has given to every scene,
By the spell of its magic power,
Some beautiful thing, if you will but heed,
Like the beautiful " Butterfly Flower."

" Las Mariposas," from which Mariposa County takes its name,
or the " Butterfly County," arises from vast tracts of these flowers,
which actually carpet, with a robe of beauty, the arid soil.

2*

LONE MOUNTAIN AND "SOPHIE."

INTRODUCTION.—Perhaps the most noticeable feature of interest at Lone Mountain Cemetery, near San Francisco, California, is a marble statue, which seems to have been a joint memorial to Christian "Faith" and Christian "Hope." There are no legends in words to enlighten the beholder while gazing on its emblematic beauty—the single word "Sophie" being all. The right foot of the female figure rests on a type of the Holy Bible, open at the 14th chapter of the Gospel of St. John, while the book lies within the anchor of Hope, or in nautical phraseology the fluke of the anchor, the cable to which is folded to the breast of the female. Around her brow is a wreath of immortelles, and on her forehead the star. The face is turned toward the Pacific Ocean, and the whole design is beautiful in conception, in execution, and in artistic grace. As the setting sun sank or seemed to sink into the ocean's bosom, and irradiated the face with its glowing tints, there on that summer eve I seemed a portion of the scene, and sitting at the feet of my divinity I sketched my ramble to the place, and paid this feeble tribute to Lone Mountain and "Sophie."

A stranger in the crowded street, a stranger from the
    mountains,
Who long had dwelt 'mid sylvan scenes, midst forests,
    rocks, and fountains;
I left the living city's haunts, where half the world was
    weeping,

And sought the city of the dead, where all seemed calmly
sleeping.

And first I climbed Lone Mountain's side, Lone Mountain, still and solemn,

To where, o'er Broderick's ashes, stands the massive gran-
ite column.

Type of the massive man who sleeps in silent loneness
under,

The son of toil, who first inspired our State with pride
and wonder.

Then down the western slope I turned, toward Magellan's Ocean,

To muse among the dead, and mark the living's deep
devotion ;

The ocean wind blew freshly o'er the graves with flowrets
laden,

Where earthly forms repose in peace, whose spirits live
in Aiden.

There bloomed the lily, pink, and rose, and beauteous
morning-glory,

And wild flowers, all beyond my lore, unknown to me in
story ;

There spirits seemed to hover o'er those who no care can
borrow,

And whispered to my troubled soul, "Here only is no
sorrow";

And birds chirped joyously around, their evening vespers
　　singing,
A deep, abiding, holy calm unto my spirit bringing.
O, ocean wind! O, summer sun! O, bird, and bud, and
　　blossom,
Ye blow, and shine, and sing, and bloom, o'er many a
　　gentle bosom;
O'er many a brain which throbs no more for glory, fame,
　　or pleasure,
For here the weary find a rest, on earth the greatest
　　treasure;
Through many an avenue and path my feet had long been
　　straying
Where marble angels meekly kneel, before the Holy
　　praying;
Until a fair and beauteous form burst on my 'wildered
　　vision,
Fair as the fairy forms I dreamed dwelt in the fields
　　Elysian.
I had been reading on the tombs of loving wife or mother
Inscriptions meant to bind the souls of earth and heaven
　　together;
But all was sacred mystery there! and nothing could
　　imply
What name the angel bore on earth, but the one word
　　"Sophie."

I know not why! a mystic thrill crept o'er me at the
   word,
I know not why! but every pulse within my being stirred,
As though my spirit-ear the voice of unseen angels heard.
Oh, loved on earth! some sorrowing friend, whose tears
   may never dry,
Hath placed thee here to gaze upon the gorgeous sunset
   sky,
And see the God of Day decline, as thou didst once,
   "Sophie!"

And I had roamed in other lands, had seen the tombs of
   kings,
And all the pomp that rank and pride round ruined
   grandeur flings;
And I had deemed them all to be but vain and senseless
   things.
Now, could my fettered spirit rise above the earth and fly,
To see what God to you reveals, but does to me deny,
I might divine the thought that wrote the single word
   "Sophie."

And round each panel then I walked, and scrutinized
   each page.

The fresh flowers bloomed beneath her feet; there was
   no sign of age.
Still, no inscription met my gaze, my fancy to engage.
I saw the book; I read the words; I know what they
   imply—
That those who trust the Savior *here*, He *there* will not
   deny;
And that with him, an angel fair, still lives the loved
   "Sophie."

There was a holy influence there—the presence of the
   dead.
It was above, it was around, it was beneath my tread.
An influence like the incense from an unseen censer shed.
Oh! that I could the mystic power unto my life ally—
The power to see the spirits round, and stand trans-
   figured by
The light I know is haloed o'er the loved on earth,
   "Sophie."

Exalted by the theme and place above all things below,
I seemed to see the spirit bands, like shadows, come
   and go,
Anon step forward, then recede, like ocean's fitful flow.
But still I think that fancy's spell is all that I can own,

The marshaling of spirit hosts belongs unto the Throne,
And till I pass the shadowy gate, to me 't is lore unknown.

    .

O, tell me! tell me! loved Sophie: while gazing o'er the
deep,
As you, beneath the vigil stars, a lonelier vigil keep,
Do not the angels, resting round, rise from their silent
sleep?
And does not here, before thy shrine, bend many a gentle
head,
Assoilzied from the taint of sin, to holy influence shed
Around thee, regal Queen of all this empire of the dead?

Across the deep, O loved Sophie! I turn my eyes to see
If ocean's bosom bears one sign to tempt my thoughts
from thee;
But all is boundless, vast expanse, from sentient being
free.
And I apostrophize the form, serenely standing by,
Could I believe, with faith supreme, of mansions in the
sky,   *
Might I with patience wait and hope? O! tell me, loved
"Sophie"!

The burnished clouds that grace the west now slowly
　　sink away,
And soon for other eyes than mine will shine the God of
　　Day.
While from Dolores Mission comes the low, sweet call to
　　pray.
And spirits whisper in my ear: You still are drawing
　　nigh.
We're near you, though ethereal forms you never can
　　descry
Till you arrive where lives in light the loved on earth,
　　"Sophie."

The anchor, "Hope," was at her feet, the "Rock of
　　Ages" there—
The rock on which no ship is wrecked, the conqueror of
　　despair.
With gaze upturned and look benign, she seemed an
　　angel fair,
So meekly pure, so sternly chaste, 't was plain she could
　　not die.
An anchorite might strive to think, and find it vain to
　　try,
To dream how stainless was the look of her, the loved
　　"Sophie."

The cable to Hope's anchor bent was folded to her breast.

The Day-God slowly sank in peace beneath the glowing
    west;

While at my feet I read the words, the words "Eternal
    Rest."

Rise, atheist, from your brutal dream, and meet my
    steadfast eye!

Tell *me* there is no life beyond, no cause for purpose
    high—

That nothing's meant by all these things, and lost is
    loved "Sophie."

San Francisco, 1875.

THE CONVICT'S BRIDE.

The scene was at the visiting-room of the State Prison, San Quentin, California. The author of this was Officer of the Day.

PART FIRST.

She sat, and in silence she waited,
　　While longing, yet dreading, to see
The lover she lately had mated,
　　When life was all careless and free.
The tears her blue eyes were suffusing,
　　Scarce hid by their lashes of brown,
And my presence I thought was abusing
　　Some sacred thought, just as a frown
Crossed her face, and her head fell before me —
　　Head weighted with wealth of brown hair,
And a sigh from her bosom upwelling
　　Showed grief near akin to despair.

What was she? the beautiful stranger,
   That she 'neath my glance seemed to cower,
As though some cloud, freighted with danger,
   Held o'er her the thrall of its power?
What was she? some Magdalen hiding
   Her face from one poor sinful man?
Or some maniac, demented by chiding,
   The world's wisdom had placed under ban?
She was—there are many thus lonely:
   Lost wrecks on the ocean of life,
Who have bartered love treasures for only
   The fate of the convict's shunn'd wife.

PART SECOND.

There's a step, and so lightly 't is falling,
   It strikes not her sensitive ear.
There's a voice, and so softly 't is calling,
   For a moment she seemed not to hear.
'T was "Dearest," and in the curst vestments
   He came from the dark prison cell—
Came forth to the sunlight and freedom,
   Where freedom was Heaven as well.
Did she shrink from the man she had wedded?

Did her eye wear the look of despair?
Was her face with the lines of grief threaded?
   Was dishevelled the wealth of her hair?
Did she bring to the loved one more sorrow,
   Augmenting his burden of care?
No.   Abandoned, she fell on his bosom,
   Her arms round his neck fondly clung.
That caress—why, 't was worth a king's ransom,
   Though the heart-strings to breaking were strung;
For him, though condemned by the many,
   There was one that was trusting and true.
One whose love was an offset for any
   And all harm the hard world could him do.
And she knew he was not the transgressor —
   'T was the demon that lurked in the wine;
In her presence he needs no confessor,
   For to him she is all that's divine.
She has seen in her vision, clear-sighted,
   The deeds of that terrible day
When the wine-cup o'ercame her own plighted,
   And one life went out in the fray.

Now back to your cell, ruined manhood,
   To wait the long, sorrowful years;
And back to your cheerless home, woman,

Your solace, the dowry of tears.
There's a taint in the air, and 't is spreading;
There's a wail, and it daily ascends;
There are thousands, now waiting and dreading
Their doom, when its influence ends
In the lives of its victims. And yet
The innocent suffer and sorrow,
And the world shows no sign of regret.

SAN QUENTIN, 1874.

FAITHLESS: A LIFE STORY.

A CONVICT'S TALE.

There are times for retrospection, when the past is
brought to view,
And we mass our faded garlands in the gardens where
they grew;
And some with rainbow hues are tinged—round some,
dark shadows play,
The first 't were well to cherish, the last to cast away.
Midst some I fondly cherish, there's one o'er which I
grieve,
Faithless! the thought is madness, born only to deceive.
And faithless one, if ever these thoughts should meet
your eye,
Think well, ere sorrows gather, of happier days gone by;
When life was in its morning, no care was on my brow,
And hope's bright day was dawning where all is darkness
now.

I thought you then a blessing, sent from the God above,
And well you know I lavished on you my all of love.
And you — you promised faithfulness, in sunshine and in
　storm,
O God! to think the serpent should find *our* Eden home.
And when they talked of perfidy, I rested in your smile,
Nor thought that one so beautiful had learned but to
　beguile.

But when the damning truth was plain, how terrible the
　hour!
The oak upon the mountain side, rent by the lightning's
　power —
The meadow, scathed by living fire, whence nothing fresh
　could start —
Was verdant to that arid waste, the desert of my heart.
I hated man, I doubted God; the future seemed to me
A lone and dreary pilgrimage on life's tempestuous sea.
Were there no other ties to bind, I then had cursed my
　race,
And placed the ocean depths between myself and your
　disgrace.
But something said, " The innocent should suffer not for
　sin :
Your helpless babes demand your care; once more the
　world begin."

To him who came between our lives I nothing then did
  say.

"Vengeance is mine"—thus saith the Lord—"I ever
  will repay."

"Sorrow at last must be the lot, the bitter lot, of those

Who make a dreary wilderness where blossomed once
  the rose."

But when he taunted me with shame, and her that gave
  me birth,

I struck him, as the wronged should strike, and felled
  him to the earth.

I know it was intent to kill; I have no guilt confessed.

I'm dying in my prison cell; your sinful life is blessed.

Willie and Johnnie I shall keep till death within my
  view;

My friends will see, if I may not, their teachings all are
  true.

Our youngest I confide to you. Oh, shelter his young
  life,

And prove the mother may be true, though faithless was
  the wife.

I've labored to forgive you long, and die without regret.

God help me to forgive you now; I never can forget.

San Quentin, 1874.

CASTE.

Before the stately edifice and all along the way,
Far as the gaze could penetrate, were equipages gay;
A flood of wealth and fashion, and diamonds brightly
　　shone
In many a matron's coiffure, and all along the zone
Of maiden youth and beauty—the city's loveliest fair;
While liveried servants flitted around the "bon ton"
　　there.
The scene was all enchantment. Within the marble walls
Were glades of tropic verdure, artistic water-falls,
While rare and prized exotics, from grand conservatoire,
Shed floods of pungent fragrance, the languid to restore.
"I must eclipse the season," the princely host has said.
"What care I for expenses? I have the fashion led,
And still propose to lead it." Now, on the joyous dance!
Where heart to heart responsive needs but the tell-tale
　　glance
To read each warm emotion—the pleasure and the joy

That consecrate these moments no pain shall here alloy.
Clear strains of thrilling music in cadence sweet are heard,
Hands clasp to love's warm pressure, by sensuous passion
    stirred;
While through the spacious chambers, with regal poise
    and stride,
Flattered, caressed, and courted, the patron walks in
    pride.

SCENE SECOND—RETROSPECTION.

Alone in his chamber, stern, silent, and gloomy,
    The Chief of the Revel sits watching the dawn.
The music has ceased, the bright wine-flow has finished,
    The chambers are silent, the guests are all gone.
There are thoughts not quite pleasant to his retrospec-
    tion,
    And there's one retribution no king can forego;
For among the bright widows who leave sad remem-
    brance
    We suspect that the worst is the "Widow Cliquot."
"Ten thousand! *ten thousand!* And gone for one party!
    With fierce opposition, and freight coming down,
And mean friends advising reform and retrenchment,
    And even the sale of my palace up town!

I've racked my brain often to find some salvation ;
   But it seems I've exhausted *all* resource, *all* chance ;
For the 'Mobilier's' dead ; so, too, 'Contract and Fi-
   nance' ;
   And the boors in the Congress no bonds will advance.
I have it ! I have it ! They're numbered by thousands—
   The dirt-begrimed toilers, the low, greasy scum.
Why, they've no use for money—do n't know how to
   use it.
   'T is reduction once more ; to my terms they must
   come.
They may growl, they may threaten, the land is o'er-
   flowing
   With labor. 'T will help me my fortunes to carve :
For the man is a fool who has lived without knowing
   The working class always give in ere they starve."

SCENE THIRD—THE NIGHT RIDE.

'T is winter, and the Storm-King reigns amid the mountains lone ;
We hear the tempest shriek and surge, in wild, discord-
   ant tone.
Or like some weird and sadd'ning dirge, wail forth a plaintive moan.

But still the Storm-King fiercely shrieks, and freely chal-
    lenge gives,

For at the time the train must go, with freight of pre-
    cious lives.

Now denser grow the deep'ning shades, the night is dark
    and drear.

Be cool! Be calm! Be steady round the curves, brave
    Engineer!

Each rivulet's a river now, each river's broadened bed

A furious, rushing torrent is, by mountain torrents fed.

A moment since we hung like flies upon the mountain's
    brow,

A thousand feet of space below: we're past that danger
    now;

But as we trembled, shook, and swayed above the fear-
    ful steep,

We felt the trestle shake, and saw a mother silent weep.

Ah! who amid the festive scene, the music, wine, and
    cheer,

Gave heed to your dear freight of life, brave, patient,
    Engineer?

Safely past the frowning mountain, where we hung upon
    its brow,

Steady! steady! nerve and valor — for we cross the tor-
    rent now.

On she glides, the iron meteor, through the Storm-King's
    realm so wild,
While the Steam-King, fiercely screaming, makes her seem
    the tempest's child;
God be thanked! the danger over, here's the station,
    bright and warm,
Now we're past the torrent's danger, and the demon of
    the storm;
And with trustful hearts and thankful, and with words of
    love and cheer,
Many tender hands grasp warmly that of the brave
    Engineer!

SCENE FOURTH— SUSPENSE AND SUFFERING.

In a cottage, sadly dreaming of a time when hope was
    beaming
As it did one summer morning, in the loved, lost long ago,
When as youth and beauty blended, in the maidens who
    attended
Her, with wealth of orange-blossoms, and a raiment white
    as snow —
As she stood before the altar, and without one sign of
    falter
She had vowed for good or evil with her best beloved
    to go —

Now, beside her children sleeping, sits the gentle mother
    weeping,

Long have passed the many moments since her husband
    should have come:

For amid all doubt and sadness there was one blest ray
    of gladness,

He had loved his wife and children, and his humble
    cottage home.

Tired, she listens for the clatter of his footsteps midst the
    patter

Of the rain-drops on the window, but she listened all
    in vain.

So, with sad forebodings teeming, sat she down to other
    dreaming.

"God have mercy! What has happened? Something
    terrible, 't is plain."

Hark! he comes, and now is knocking loudly, wildly,
    and the shocking

Truth's apparent to the mother that the wine-fiend has
    been there;

And she bowed, and said in sorrow, "God preserve us
    till the morrow.

Something awful has succeeded that he thus dispels de-
    spair."

Spake he, "Oh, my love, my peerless, was not your lone
    home so cheerless,

Quite enough to make a tyrant's heart have pity on the
    poor?

Quite enough to give the pittance that would scarcely
    bar admittance

To the demons Want and Hunger from our humble cot-
    tage door? .

No. The grasping corporations, curses to all toil's rela-
    tions,

Have again proclaimed, 'Reduction,' drowning hope
    forever more.

God of Mercy, God of Justice, in whose help our only
    trust is,

Now forgive the fearful lesson we this night have sworn
    to give.

Well Thou knowest, strong and tender, that no class
    should blaze in splendor,

While the toilers who have made them are denied the
    means to *live.*"

SCENE FIFTH—RETRIBUTION.

Fire! fire!! fire!!!
Like a horror it strikes the ear;
And the brave and true in the battle's van,
Where the foe is simply a mortal man,
Succumb to a sense of fear.

For the children's cry and the women's wail
Heralds the old, the oft-told tale,
As the tongues of flame rise higher! higher!
While the whistle's shriek and the clang of bells
The tale of the tyrant's conquests tells
Of burning cities and seething hells!
Midst the terrible cry of Fire! Fire! Fire!!

SCENE SIXTH—THE SEQUEL.

From his stately palace window looks the author of the
    drama
On the blazing scene of horror—on the scene of strife
    below.
Where is now the helpless toiler? Answer! Answer!
    Arch Despoiler—
Of the only real *safeguard* this our boasted land can
    know.
'T was not cannon, lance, or saber—no!—'t was paid,
    enlightened labor
That built up the wondrous greatness seen at our Cen-
    tennial show.
Power nor wealth can save this nation—never wealth
    in concentration—
While a righteous compensation is to labor's hand denied.

Citizens, not serfs, are wanted. Men whose minds by
   whips are haunted

Never can uphold our honor—be unto the land a pride.

History speaks! a child can read it. History speaks, and
   men should heed it.

'T is no problem! all its lessons the most simple may
   divine;

Show the mills of God grind slowly—grind the lofty as
   the lowly:

When from right a people wander, God still says " Re-
   venge is mine."

3*

THE REIGN OF PUBLIC OPINION.

"Sir! The time is fast approaching when Public Opinion shall
be stronger than kings and emperors; when public sympathy shall
be mightier than armies and navies."—*Webster, Speech on the Greek
Revolution*, 1824.

Has it come? It has come, and the tyrants well know it,
　　And the world must soon bow to its sway;
Though the sentiment passed all unheeded, unnoticed,
　　Half a century before us to-day.
It was seen with prevision to God's only second,
　　By the Sage who men's deeper thoughts knew,
And when once on the minds of the thoughtful it rested,
　　How proudly it flourished and grew !
Under God it shall grow, till the gage of the combat
　　Is left not to sword or to lance—
Till Public Opinion, by reason enlightened,
　　Shall herald refinement's advance.
And the millions no more shall be crushed to the earth
By the glitter of riches or prestige of birth.

Take heed then, ye despots! the word has been spoken,
    Old creeds and old issues shall fall,
When Public Opinion pronounces unhallowed
    The forms that enchain and enthral.
'Tis decreed in the land that one power, and one only,
    Under God shall our destinies lead :
The power that preserved, and defended, and guarded—
    That power is the People—take heed!
In the halls of the Nation that power, represented,
    Shall speak, and the mandate go forth ;
'T will be heard in the East, and the West, and the South
    Land,
    'T will resound from the hills of the North :
That the millions no more shall be crushed to the earth
By the glitter of riches or prestige of birth.

That power showed its might when the war tempest
    gathered
    Like the storm on the wild, raging main ;
When the tramp of armed hosts drove sweet Peace from
    our borders,
    And fraternal blood poured like the rain.
When Freedom resplendent in triumph upreared,
    While her blazing sword shone in the sun ;
When our eagle's fierce glance almost quailed in its light

As she swore we should ever be One,
And the millions no more should be crushed to the earth
By the glitter of riches or prestige of birth.

Advance then, ye millions! from mental enthrallment,
  With the gods of advancement to soar,
Till Public Opinion, refined and ennobled,
  Shall know degradation no more;
Till forth from the bench, and the loom, and the anvil,
  Are sparkles of intellect brought,
And no class and no caste shall presume for dominion
  Amid the high regions of thought.
Then shall Labor ennobled be King of the World,
  And the mighty before it shall bow,
When its banner, the emblem of progress, unfurled,
  Shall emblazon the pick, plane, and plow.
Then the millions no more shall be crushed to the earth
By the glitter of riches or prestige of birth.

THE PRINCESS WIEMAR:

A LEGEND OF THE GOLDEN AGE.

I had roamed the wide world over,
   I had sailed on every sea;
Tropic clime, or Borean region,
   Each were commonplace to me.

Belles had sought to win my homage,
   Sought to win me by their smile;
But my heart was cold as winter,
   I had learned the ways of guile.

I had read the " Tales of Cooper ";
   Read of " radiant Indian Queens "
In the mountains' stately forests—
   On the valleys' lovely greens.

No! no common love should win me—
City life was tame and slow;
I would woo and wed a princess—
To the wild-wood I would go.

So I left the town and market
For the mountain and the mine,
In the Golden Age's birth time,
In the year of Forty-Nine.

From its course we turned the river,
Where for ages it had rolled,
And my comrades all were happy,
For its bed was sown with gold.

But my heart was dead within me;
Every day the same routine.
I had met no forest beauty,
I had seen no " Indian Queen."

Months had passed—'t was Indian summer,
And the south wind's gentle breath
Came, the soft and sweet forerunner
Of the year's approaching death.

When I left my camp and comrades,
   Wandered forth among the hills :
Faded were the summer's glories,
   Dried the spring-time's gushing rills.

And the sighing of the zephyrs
   Through the pine-trees seemed to say,
With a sad Æolian cadence,
   " Passing, passing all away."

Suddenly, as if by magic,
   Stood before my sight arrayed
One more grand realization
   Than my fancy had portrayed.

She was dressed—I 'll drop the fashion—
   But her lovely shoulders bore
One red blanket, somewhat dingy,
   Simply that, and nothing more.

It was fastened round her bosom,
   Just above the tawny zones,
By some San Diego diamonds
   Made from shells of abalones.

Oh, the glory of her coiffure!
  On the theme I long could dwell;
No chignon, but pitch and ashes,
  With a terebinthine smell.

Oh, the simple child of nature!
  How she bore my earnest gaze,
With a trusting unsuspicion
  Rare in these degenerate days.

On her back she bore her dowry—
  Flattened out upon a board
Hung the heir of all the Pi-Utes—
  He was gagged and never stirred.

I had learned from friend **Longfellow**
  How the noble savage died,
With a silent, unrelenting,
  Fierce, ungovernable pride.

There I learned to solve the puzzle—
  Early training was the trick;
That young brave could die by inches,
  But could neither cry nor kick.

Quickly she unloosed her burden,
    Flung it down beside a rock;
Think of that, Caucasian mothers,
    Who have feeble nerves to shock.

Then I asked the peerless beauty
    What her Indian name might be;
And she answered, "Wine-tum-sam-shew
    Ho-lo-ting-muck-Na-goo-chee."

So 't was plain she was a princess,
    And could my devotion claim;
With the Indian—as the white man—
    Lineage goes by length of name.

But the night was growing colder,
    And the stars began to shine;
What was there that I could do for
    One so lovely—so divine?

Quickly, then, as if by instinct,
    I a flask of brandy drew;
And I offered that unto her—
    Wonderful! how well she knew!

Pious men, we Forty-Niners!
　We who have not fortunes made,
For we never think of striving
　Without spiritual aid.

Oh, the magnitude of swallow!
　Oh, the volume of the draught!
When I saw her so accomplished,
　Cupid launched the fatal shaft.

In a cañon near the Carson,
　From the city's vice away—
Where the white man's missing cattle
　Unaccountably do stray—

You may find a red " campoodie,"
　And within a redder face;
There I keep my Indian beauty,
　There I rear my dusky race.

They shall never know the troubles
　That attend on books and schools;
Never know the vain repinings
　Of the educated fools.

Never follow politicians
  For the sake of filthy gain,
And find out that modern greatness
  Builds on truth, and mankind slain.

Never tread the Senate chambers,
  And descend to take a bribe—
Shaming all the honest record
  Of the Pi-Ute Indian tribe.

Better track the gaunt coyote,
  Chase the wild, impetuous hare,
Hunt to death the fierce hog-squirrel,
  Run before the grizzly bear,

Ride a noble mustang pony,
  And of manhood loudly brag;
While the light of all the harem
  Walks behind, and packs the "swag."

Bad, indeed, these savage instincts,
  Undefiled by love of gold;
Worse, to sell a trusting people,
  And themselves to shame be sold.

THE SCHOOLMA'AM'S LETTER·

OR

RETROSPECTION.

———

I have your letter, little friend,
   And from it catch a ray,
A charm, to holy influence lend
   And cheer my lonely way.

You talk of duty and of toil,
   And you so young to rule;
Now, I, grown old in life's turmoil,
   To you will go to school.

I see a trusting candor there,
   It breathes from every line;
I know the inner life is fair,
   I catch the ray divine.

And, as I seem to hear your tones,
   A voice responsive sings :
" On earth there still are stepping-stones
   Which lead to higher things."

So through the intervening years
   I cast the gloom away,
And all the sorrows, doubts, and fears
   That once obscured my way.

The spirit harp, which long had slept,
   To music now is strung ;
Its heavenly influence I accept,
   And, as of yore, I'm young.

I know you are not present here,
   And still your form I see ;
What is the mirror, little friend,
   That shadows only thee?

I'll tell you—and perchance I know—
   My life has lonely been ;
All that's of value here below
   Exists in the unseen.

The unseen power—to comprehend
  The unseen beauty, spread
Not only in the heavenly realm,
  But *here*, beneath our tread.

The unseen power—to summon back
  From memory's garnered store
The flowers that bloomed upon our track
  In halcyon days of yore.   .

And so, my little one, I here
  The new impulse will tell;
Brought forth again, without a fear,
  Beneath your magic spell.

I am once more a boy again,
  And roam the meadows gay,
In childhood's home, in distant Maine,
  Beside my queenly May.

For Mary was the maiden's name—
  My sainted mother's, too—
And you to make the triad came:
  The mirror shadows true.

Your letter brought the clover blooms,
   The meadow and the flowers;
It was the sunshine midst the glooms,
   The rainbow midst the showers.

It brought the church, the village spire,
   The school-house in the lane,
And, what is more, a strong desire
   To see those scenes again.

It brought them by the simple words
   Of " duty " and of "rule";
For my May Queen in distant Maine
   Reigned o'er the village school.

Accept this simple offering, dear,
   'T is all that age can give;
But while the roses cluster near,
   The oak will try to live.

               To M. F. G.

ODE TO THE COMSTOCK ENGINEERS.

Here—where our Imperial City
   Towers above the valley lands,
And Mount Davidson, the Monarch,
   Like an ancient giant stands;
Sentinel of all the ages,
   Who has seen the waters flow,
Heard the night wind's shrieks and dirges
   Many a thousand years ago—
Who is first to greet the Sun-God
   Rising from Aurora's breast;
Last to feel his warm caresses,
   Sinking in the burnished West—
Here we meet for new communion,
   All the friends of former years,
To you each a hearty greeting,
   Friends and brother Engineers.

Yes! my friends, through cycled ages,
   Since this world had life and birth—
Since its burning cauldron, cooling,

Made for man a home on earth—
Since a troglodyte man wandered,
Lived with wild beast in its lair—
None had come to claim the treasure,
None had dared its gloom to share.
Science broke the mighty barrier,
And the bullion outward flows,
Making all the desert blossom
With a beauty like the rose.
But it still would be the desert
That it was a million years,
Were it not for our profession,
Friends and brother Engineers.

'T is our hands that guide the motor,
Make the arm of iron play,
Hold the Steam-King in dominion
Ceaselessly, by night and day.
Guard the miner, while he quarries
From the depths the shining ore,
Richer than the costly lading
Of the argosies of yore.
We! who guide the reel and cable,
Balance the ascending cage;
Actors in the world of progress,
In this grand, progressive age.

4

Many a household in the city
    Would be filled with grief and tears
Were we false to our commission,
    Friends and brother Engineers.

Where the wild Pi-Ute wandered
    Through the long and dreary whiles,
Now are heard the strains of music,
    Now we're cheered by woman's smiles.
Woman! Man's supreme evangel,
    Comes to meet us here to-night ;
Let us greet earth's wingless angel,
    Type on earth of forms of light!
She has blessed us by her presence,
    And her smile our meeting cheers :
For the time forget all trouble,
    Friends and brother Engineers.

Recited by the Hon. J. E. Coulter before the Fraternity of Stationary Engineers of the Comstock, at their Annual Ball, Virginia City, 1878.

THE MINER'S FLAG.

1862.

What glory meets the miner's eyes
  When morning light appears,
Braces his arm to sturdy toil,
  His manly bosom cheers?
It is his country's glorious flag
  Waving from yon old pine,
To keep alive the ardent hopes
  Which round his heart entwine.
His hardy hand has placed it there
  On yon majestic tree,
Fit emblem of the patriot heart,
  Reliant, bold, and free.

What though the fabric is not made
  Of silken tissues fine?
What though no balls of gold or gilt
  High in the sunlight shine?

'T was not for vanity or show
　They flung it to the breeze;
'T was made not by the minions
　Of power, or wealth, or ease.
Fair hands as any in the land
　Have lent to it their charm,
And round it cling as holy hopes
　Affections pure and warm.
And *men* will guard and keep it there,
　Yon pine tree waving o'er,
Until unstained, unstainable,
　" 'T is the old flag of yore ! "

The Druid at his altar,
　The Gheber at his fires,
Felt not a purer, holier thrill
　Than that our flag inspires
In those who, true to duty,
　Humanity and God,
Have sworn to follow in the path
　Our patriot fathers trod,
And keep on high that banner—
　To tyrants all a ban—
Since the Messiah's advent
　God's greatest gift to man.

The pine tree that supports our flag
  Was nurtured midst the rocks;
Has borne the summer's scorching heat,
  The winter's tempest shocks;
And hands of man have from it torn
  Full many a gallant arm,
Yet still it lives, all fresh and green,
  Invincible to harm.
And should within the Golden State
  Foul treason rear its head,
Or should a traitor's impious foot .
  Within its shadow tread,
We'll reeve upon its topmost branch
  A girt-line, strong and true,
To show what patriot hearts can dare,
  What patriot hands can do.
And there his festering corse shall hang,
  Our loved flag waving o'er,
Till Treason, banished, quits the State,
  From mountain crest to shore.

POEM DELIVERED AT CARSON CITY,

JULY 4th, 1877.

INVOCATION.

Not to "paint the rainbow brighter,"
Not to gild this morning's glory,
Not to build a fragile frost-work
 That shall melt and fade away.
Not alone by show and pageant,
Flaunting plumes, barbaric splendor,
Cloth of gold or sheen of diamonds,
 Can we consecrate this day.
On the land some still are weeping
 For the loved ones gone before us ;
On the land the maimed are lingering,
 Showing what the war once bore us.
Now the past and present meet us,
Now the new-born century greets us,
 While we glory still we pray;
Pray that Freedom, consecrated

By the tears of weeping millions—
By the life-blood of the Nation
Freely offered on its altar—
May from us be parted—never!
May with us forever stay!

POEM.

No! No hollow gilded pageant first announced this
Nation's birth;
Feebly rose that constellation which already lights the
earth.
Now! from North-land, with its shadows and its clouds
of murky hue;
Now! from South-land's green savannahs, where the
skies are ever blue;
From bleak plain and sheltered forest, river's side and
shaded dell,
From the East and from the West-land—see the human
ocean swell!
From the tropic seas and islands, where the spikes of
coral grow;
From the mountains hyperborean, crested o'er with tops
of snow;
From our own Nevada's hillsides, where a wealth of
treasure lies

That would purchase all the fruitage ripened under tropic
    skies ;
From the vales of new Arcadias, all unknown in days of
    yore,
To this annual celebration—see Columbia's children pour,
While the stars, that once were waning, proudly to the
    zenith soar.

Like an ocean overflowing to bring forth a grander sea,
Is to-day the mighty gathering of the millions of the free,
Shadowing forth the unknown grandeur of the empire yet
    to be.
If among the gathered millions, like Assyrian king of old,
There are those who think our prestige can be raised or
    changed by gold,
I shall charge them to remember God was never bought
    or sold.
Centuries of grief and suffering, gales of sighs and floods
    of tears
Were the price of our great dowry—all the hope of com-
    ing years.
Not for present exaltation have the earnest millions met,
But to keep alive the memories they have sworn not to
    forget ;
And to reassure the doubters, at this new-born century's
    dawn,

That its finish will accomplish more than all the centuries
    gone.
Shades of thee! O patriot fathers! if the ransomed ever
    stray
From the realms of light and glory, minister with us
    to-day.
Shades of thee! our late defenders, who have died the
    boon to save,
Lend us thy supernal presence, from the realm beyond
    the grave.
Muse of History! we invoke thee! o'er us now thy
    mantle cast;
While we here rehearse the struggles and the triumphs
    of the past,
Show when o'er her own dominion Freedom's horoscope
    was cast.
While we prove that truth eternal, that no casuist ever
    hides—
"That however man proposes, it is ever God who guides."
Show that, midst that constellation, One—the First—the
    Leading Star,
Saved through centuries of darkness, famine, pestilence
    and war,
Is the Star to Bethlehem followed from the plains of old
    Shinar.

THE CENTENNIAL YEAR.

FOURTH OF JULY, 1876.

In the Old World was darkness! The people were bowed
In most abject submission! No rift broke the cloud.
Dread tyranny triumphed on land and on sea,
And heart to heart whisp'ring asked, Can man be free
From the toils of the despots? In darkness and night
The political victim's shriek broke in affright
From some bastile's deep dungeon! The fierce lurid fire
Encompassed some victim for faith to expire
In agonized torture! And God's face from the path
Of the truthful and just seemed withdrawn in his wrath.
In the lands of the East, cursed with mildew and blight,
Where for ages stern Might had been lord of the Right,
Hope seemed fled from the earth! And men prayed in
    despair
To their God for some succor, some proof of his care.
No, none! 'T was the gibbet, the dungeon, and stake,
The tides of the ocean, the fetter, and brake.

No mercy, no ruth, king or bigot could feel—
'T was the conscienceless rack and the merciless wheel;
Till, despairing of hope in the East to find rest,
A few of God's chosen sailed forth for the West:
Sailed forth on the winter-bound, tempest-tossed sea,
To engulf in its bosom, or live grandly free.
What perils they passed on their long, lonely way,
Are passed, and we stand, their descendants, to-day
To rejoice in the triumphs and victories won
By the martyrs to freedom in ages long gone.

COLONIZATION—1620.

Away! away! in the far East, past where our mountains
    soar,
We see a frail and feeble bark, a surf-washed, rock-bound
    shore;
A savage coast, with savage men — an aspect stern and
    wild,
A snowy mantle, winter-spread, the cradle for our child!
And one by one, we see them there droop, fall, and
    patient die:
Has God, who guarded o'er the deep, withdrawn His
    watchful eye?

Again we see a chosen few recross the stormy main
To find some help the feeble germ of freedom to maintain;
And succor came, though tardily, to save the dying
      germ,
And bless exulting millions here, in this the exile's
      home.

THE COLONISTS.

Time passed, and the young giant throve, and strong and
      sturdy grew,
But still to the old Mother-Land was faithful, firm, and
      true;
A lion in his sinewy strength, an eagle in his glance,
We fought for Britain savage foes, and veteran troops of
      France.
But still the Mother-Land knew not—so sternly, strangely
      cold —
That only silken cords can lead the valiant, young, and
      bold.
And though with all of filial love they loved the old home
      well,
There is a point when even love 'gainst outrage must
      rebel.

THE DECLARATION OF INDEPENDENCE.

'T was then! above the fear of death, to God and free-
dom true,
They met for protest and appeal, the brave and honored
few,   .
The chosen sons of freedom: all honor to the men!
Failure was ignominious death! they knew the verdict
then.'
In solemn conclave still they met, declared that "man is
free,"
Announced the truth that always was, and is, and yet
shall be—
That man is born the peer of man by God's divine decree.
They met to combat, then and there, the right divine of
kings,
The base assumption that the mass of men are simply
things,
With right to nothing but the dole that base subjection
brings.
Moved by one impulse then they did the deed none
shall recall,
The deed we celebrate to-day. Hail to those patriots all!

WAR OF THE REVOLUTION.

Of the long bloody fight that came, 't were idle here to
　　show—
'T is graven on each patriot heart—even the children
　　know
How the first fight, on Bunker's height, was sounded o'er
　　the land;
How, thrilled by Henry's eloquence, Virginia took her
　　stand;
How Iron Putnam, Allen, Stark, were giants in the
　　North;
How Marion, Sumpter, Rutledge, Lee, immortalized the
　　South;
And how, though feeble, poor, and few, for eight long,
　　weary years
Undaunted and invincible, they fought, through blood
　　and tears,
Until Columbia's soil became a second Marathon,
While far above all Grecians towered immortal Washing-
　　ton!

WAR OF 1812.

Again we fought the ancient foe, upon her field, the
main ;

St. George's cross some prestige lost — we won our cause
again.

With proud Britannia held our own, queen of a thousand
fights,

And vindicated honor's cause, " Free Trade and Sailors'
Rights ! "

The Old World wondered — stood amazed — to see the
infant power

Cope with the mistress on the main, which she had held
as dower

Since the Armada's boasted fleet, the haughty Spaniard's
pride,

Was dashed in pieces on her coast, and choked her
channel's tide.

Of fratricidal conflict now, we speak not—let it rest ;

We all have suffered, and we hope the future may be
blest.   •

The reign of peace we hail !

The strife is past—we bow, and throw its ashes to the
gale ;

Columbia's genius hovers near—exultant now she sings:
Now listen to the song of peace, the message that she
brings:

TRIUMPHS.

"In the century that's past I have triumphed at last,
  And with pride saw my wonder-land grow
From the islands of green, in the tropic seas seen,
  To the northern isles crested with snow;
Saw the lightnings of heaven from the cloudlet unriven,
  To be subject and part of your dower,　　　　·
And I hear the fierce steam a bound captive now scream,
  The chained servant of progress and power."

  *   *   *   *   *

"Children, wisdom now is wanting! not an idle useless
  vaunting
Of our progress as a nation or our present matchless
  powers—
Wisdom so to mould the present that ambitions evanes-
  cent
Which destroyed the old republics may not curse this
  land of ours.
Yes! that wisdom, pure and simple, which o'er human
  wisdom towers.

'T is the spring-time makes the reaping a rejoicing or a
weeping:

Says the word of God Eternal: 'Ye shall harvest what
is sown.'

Sow, then, at the century's dawning, in this fair and
radiant morning,

What shall bless the unknown future when the harvest
shall be mown.

Nature's mysteries, now unveiling, show that science,
never failing,

Soon may learn the hidden secrets of this earth from pole
to pole,

Show God has no lore so hidden that it will not come
when bidden

By that mystery of our being—God's eternal gift, the soul.

Revelation's old unfoldings all result in new beholdings,

Before which the mysteries vanish as the night-gloom
flees the day;

And the present scintillations of the most unseen creations

By that soul-power shall be mirrored ere the century
fades away.

Seekers for the unseen kingdom, pleasant are the ways
of wisdom;

Stop not, quail not, till the fetters that bind down the
mind are riven.

Death will leave where birth-time found them, nations, if
not woven round them,

As the one eternal dowry which the God of Light has
given.

Wisdom never was an earth-power. Wisdom never was
an earth-dower.

Wisdom born of earthly knowledge dies when dies
earth's fading day.

Where all earthly knowledge slumbers, lie those nations'
countless numbers

Who have lost the priceless dowry, 'God the talent took
away.'

Heed not, spurn the base deceivers; heed not all the
unbelievers,

Who would rob you of that guerdon, that, the sum of
riches all.

Give you all that earth can give you, give you what at
death will leave you

Where each nation rests who listened not to Wisdom's
spirit call."

MORAL.

The skeptic and the scoffer laughed when once the Master said

That every idle word should be by Omnipresence read.

Now science proves the knowledge true that Christ to
    scoffers spoke,
For symboled words foretold the doom that broke Bel-
    shazzar's yoke
Ages before, when he assumed to be the lord of all;
And forth the mystic warning came, handwritten on the
    wall.
And since, no nation lived in peace, from ages most
    remote,
Who boasted God's prerogative. 'T was God's own hand
    that wrote;
And Wisdom wrote what Wisdom knew, the wherefore
    and the when;
For nations are but aggregates of all the types of men.
And judgment comes when nations mass their faults
    and truths forget;
No nation ever tried the scheme and lives in safety yet.
Egypt, Assyria, Greece, and Rome have found their age
    of gloom,
And other nations linger near the portals of their tomb.

And History echoes in our ears,
  Borne down the aisles of time,
" God will preserve what Wisdom rears—
  Children, be wise in time !"

DAN. v: 24.

COLUMBIA, MY COUNTRY.

Columbia, my country! The last born of nations,
   The herald of freedom, the Star of the West,
The brightest of stars midst the earth's constellations,
   Still on thy broad bosom mankind shall be blest.
Long dispersed are the clouds that rebellion once gath-
   ered,
   And to dim thy resplendence no mists intervene;
Your old " Ship of State" all the tempests has weath-
   ered,
   And your zenith in beauty glows calm and serene.

Columbia, my country! The world knows your story—
   How tyrants to crush you essayed in your youth.
You arose from the conflict with honor and glory,
   And proved to the despots the prowess of truth.
Men sprang from oppression its fetters to sunder,
   Asserting the rights made immortal by mind,
While, speechless, the tyrants gazed on you in wonder,
   The refuge, the glory, the hope of mankind.

Columbia, my country! Your flag has been floating
   For years in prosperity, glory, and peace,
While o'er its proud luster your true sons were gloating,
   Rejoicing its blessings and power to increase.
But the slime of one serpent was over it trailing,
   In the North-land and South-land, engendering strife,
While the good and the true its foul course was bewailing,
   It stung the fair bosom that warmed it to life.

Then Columbia, my country, as springs from the ocean
   The wild, maddened sprays 'neath the hurricane's blast,
Your faithful and loyal sprang forth from your bosom
   And swore the foul heresy never should last;
That your flag, once degraded, insulted, and humbled,
   Should again in the sunlight unstainable shine,
While the recreants who sought to forever debase it
   Should perish in shame at their infamous shrine.

'T was done! and, Columbia, your grandeur transcending
   All Nature achieved for the climes of the East,
Your mountains, your rivers, your forests, all tending
   In spell-bound enchantment the senses to feast,
Inspire in each bosom pure love and devotion,
   And kindle within us a soul-stirring flame;
Your shores ever washed by the waves of each ocean,
   A continent proudly exults in your name.

Columbia, my country! I love your cold regions,
   The home of my childhood, the place of my birth.
Temptations are powerless, though counted by legions,
   To make me forget that one spot on the earth.
But I love your calm South, with her sunny savannas,
   I love your stern East, near Atlantic's unrest,
And I love—yes, adore—with its sunshine and shadows,
   Your beauteous, resplendent, and wealth-giving West!

Columbia, my country! No myths or traditions
   Did your birth and your infancy ever obscure;
You arose on the ruins of old superstitions
   At the dawn of an era whose promise is sure.
We claim not the fabled "St. George and the Dragon,"
   St. Michael of Russia, St. Dennis of France,
Or the gods of the pagans, Astarte or Dagon—
   We trust the Almighty to guide our advance.

Columbia, my country! With luster undying
   Your banner in glory and honor sustained—
The base machinations of all foes defying,
   Your eagle high soaring in might unrestrained—
Now that sweet Peace is beaming from ocean to ocean.
   Again highly prospered, by Providence blest—
The hearts of your children swell high with devotion,
   And proudly exult in their "Star of the West."

SUPERCILIOUS AIRS:

OR

THE MINER'S SURPRISE.

———

Attend, ye sons of labor all,
  While I a tale will tell—
A small adventure which of late
  My humble self befell.

And know, before I tell the tale—
  This simple tale of mine —
I represent the " Prodigals "
  Who came in Forty-nine.

'T was on a hill, near by the town,
  Where once the wildwood grew ;
Where tangled shrubs and trailing vines
  Hung glistening in the dew.

Primeval Nature reigned supreme,
   And all was calm and still,
Save where some lonely rocker plied
   Beside the murmuring rill.

The miner sang and rocked the soil
   From morn till daylight's close,
Till from his strength and sturdy toil
   This beauteous town arose.

The forest trees have passed away;
   Scarce one of all remains.
The mountain soil is gaily clothed
   With verdure from the plains.

And cottages, with taste ornate,
   Stand where tall trees did grow;
And where the wild flowers bloomed unseen
   Do cultured roses blow.

Midst humble dwellings scattered round,
   There stands *one* grander still,
Within a spacious garden placed—
   The Palace of the Hill.

5

Unto its portal once of late
   I strolled its lord to see,
And there the small adventure met
   Which you shall hear from me.

For, as I wandered down the lane,
   Before I was aware,
I met a nymph with dainty hat
   And supercilious air.

My mining clothes, so much like those
   ' I wore in Forty-nine,
Caused such surprise unto her eyes
   She could not me divine.

She turned—a dull and stony look
   Of scorn on me she threw,
And with a most superb disdain
   Departed from my view.

Among the grass the withered leaves
   Seemed more intensely dead;
The gravel stones that paved the walk
   Recoiled beneath her tread.

The wind, which silent was till then,
　Wailed forth a plaintive moan,
And whirled before her feet away
　The leaves which it had strewn.

The pigeon pets that graced the cote
　Withdrew before her glance;
The house-cat round the corner peered,
　Then fled from her advance.

All nature seemed to feel the shock—
　The sun withdrew his face,
Shamed to see supercilious pride
　Spoil beauty, youth, and grace.

Perchance the lady did not know,
　Of supercilious air,
That to provide that dainty hat
　The miner paid a share.

Perchance the lady did not know
　That maze of crinoline
Was bought with gold that miners' hands
　Brought from the dark unseen.

Perhaps she thought that golden dust
　Would flow into her hand
Without the sturdy sons of toil,
　The miners of the land.

Ah, lady ! Well the mansion looks,
　The gardens bright and fair ;
But spare for drones and city knaves
　Your supercilious air.

The diamond is a diamond still—
　A pure and peerless gem—
In the dark, lonesome caves of earth,
　A regal diadem.

The same in solitude and gloom,
　As when, the sport of chance,
It gleams from beauty's radiant brow
　Amid the mazy dance.

The flowret changes not its hue
　To please the gazer's eye,
And sheds the same perfume for all,
　The lowly or the high.

The song-bird varies not its note
To please the listener's ear,
But pours harmonious melody
That all may freely hear.

Ye graceful and ye beautiful,
For God's dear love forbear
To look upon the sons of toil
With supercilious air;

Lest we, deprived of human love
While on this earthly sod
By God's most holy masterwork,
Forget all love to God.

NEVADA COUNTY, CALIFORNIA, 1856.

NATURE'S DOWER.

To a Young Lady who asked what were the Writer's
Possessions and Patrimony.

Where, do you ask, are my acres paternal ?
    What can I bring to your hand ?
What is the dowry reserved for the bridal ?
    Where are the realms I command ?
This is the portion bequeathed by my father,
    All my domain, where I stand.

That is *my* brook, which the meadow enlivens,
    Decked with its margins of green ;
Hold I *my* castles where snow-crested mountains,
    Stately, high-towering are seen ;
There ! where the turrets to heaven up-reaching,
    Gleam in the sun's golden sheen.

Those are my gems, ever pure and resplendent,
  Strung in the firmament's dome;
Brightly they glisten with luster unfading,
  Luring my spirit to home:
Never a watchman I need to protect them,
  Robbers of light never come.

See ye my statues?   Antique are the models,
  Known to the ancients of yore.
Groves were the temples where men first did worship,
  First did their Maker adore,
When o'er the aisles of the forest primeval
  Smoke from the altar did soar.

Where are the minstrels that joy to delight me,
  Breathing their souls into song?
There! where the brook bubbles forth from the grotto,
  Sweetly their lays they prolong.
Nature's wild warblers—the lark and the linnet—
  Far from the world's busy throng.

Where are the paintings my chambers adorning,
  Breathing of beauty divine?
See ye the wild flowers that hang from the creepers?
  Art can but copy their line;

Matchless in tint, and in splendor effulgent,
  They all the graces combine.

See ye the rainbow, the child of refraction,
  Born from the affluence of light?
See ye the bright burnished clouds of the sunset,
  Fairer than fancy's proud flight?
Art's highest labors appear in the contrast
  Clothed in the darkness of night.

Bring me one guerdon—'t is all I solicit;
  Help all these gifts to employ:
Wanting that help, earth a wilderness seemeth;
  With it, bliss hath no alloy.
Then shall we find as earth's borders we travel
  Ceaseless the sources of joy.

Bring me the charm that, in sympathy blending,
  Looks to the regions above;
Those who can see not the bounties of Heaven
  Know not its lessons of love.
Then will my heart ope its portals to greet you,
  And the Ark will make welcome the Dove.

NEVADA CITY, 1860.

"NO LICENSE!"—TO PAVE THE DARK PATHWAY TO HELL.

The slogan is sounding!—all hail! brothers hail!
By the mountains 't is echoed—'t is borne on the gale;
The dark clouds are lifting—the mists clear away,
And soon through their rifting will shine the bright day
What, what is the watchword that floats on the air,
That with rose-tint of hope gilds the clouds of despair?
'T is "No license!" the death-dealing liquid to sell!
'T is "No license!" to pave the dark pathway to hell!

An l whence comes the promise that rests on the air,
That with rose-tint of hope gilds the clouds of despair?
Was it born in the halls of the wealthy or great?
Did it spring from the mentors who rule for the state?
Or from "public opinion," which claims to be right,
Did it spring in full armor, resplendently bright?
No! never such glory their fame did yet swell
As no license to pave the dark pathway to hell!

It was born from oppression; 'twas nurtured in grief,
Till from suffering and sorrow it sprang for relief;
Like Gethsemane's martyr, from almost despair
It arose to the light, on the pinions of prayer;
And the wail of the millions, who sorrowed alone,
Now breaks in one billow, now swells in one tone,
And this is the judgment 'tis destined to tell —
"No license!" to pave the dark pathway to hell!

Arise in your manhood—to duty come forth;
Let the land of the sunset respond to the north—
For woman has bowed before God and the throne,
And led where proud man dared not travel alone.
Fulfill the requirement! and meet the decree,
And henceforth from the wine-fiend's dominion be free.
Let it sound in the ears of the tyrant a knell,
"No license!" to pave the dark pathway to hell!

No license! No license! Oh, brothers take heed!
No license! to further make broken hearts bleed!
No license! No license! Raise high the acclaim,
No license! to pander to falsehood and shame.
'Tis the first dawning ray in the fullness of time,
No license for murder, no license for crime;
No license to purchase, to make, or to sell,
No license to pave the dark pathway to hell!

The Goddess of Freedom, with courage sublime,
Has just vanquished one monster that threatened her
    clime;
Now her eye, fiercely blazing, sees on her loved sod
Another! that trifles with freedom and God.
It was not God or nature that placed on the earth
A *curse* so abnormal, so monstrous in birth,
As the life-stealing, death-dealing, soul-scathing well,
That flows onward to people the region of hell!

Oh, guides to salvation! ye priests of the cross,
Have you studied the question? the gain and the loss?
Have you weighed the temptation to sin in the wine,
When none but the pure can on Jesus recline?
Heed not your false prophets, plead not for the sin,
Which from little beginnings destruction will win.
If the doctrine of Jesus you wish to preach well,
Preach No license! to pave the dark pathway to hell!

'T is summer! The gardens are painted in bloom,
And the zephyrs of evening are breathing perfume;
All nature is resting, the bliss seems profound,
As if earth-land and cloud-land elysium had found.
Hark! Hark! There's a cry! There's a shriek on the air!
'T is murder! foul murder! a wail of despair!

No matter! there's license the liquor to sell,
There is license to pave the dark pathway to hell.

'Tis winter, and midnight, and fierce howls the blast,
And the storm from the ocean drives furious and fast;
And a form, once of beauty, flits noiselessly by—
There is death in her pallor, despair in her eye;
Before, the dark river floats turbidly on—
There's a shriek, and a plunge, and a victim has gone
To join the lost millions; oh, friends, is it well
Still further to pave the dark pathway to hell?

Oh! toilers of earth! In this land of the free
It is yours to redeem if redeemed we shall be.
Our banner is waving—come, now, join the ranks,
And to God will your wives and your children give thanks.
No longer your heart-broken loved ones shall weep:
We are strong to redeem you and stronger to keep.
Swell the tide of advancement—with us come and dwell,
And license no more the dark pathway to hell.

'Tis the gift of the ages by progress brought down,
'Tis the present's best guerdon our glory to crown.
Break the maniac's foul fetters, the captive set free,
Let forever be banished the cursed gallows-tree.

Let the senator's judgment be calm and serene,
Let the ermine of justice from baseness be clean,
And consign to oblivion in darkness to dwell,
The *time* when was licensed a pathway to hell.

Then the mountains shall echo, the valleys shall ring,
And the isles of the ocean their offerings shall bring,
And the dower of the ages, the land of the West,
Shall be truly and proudly the land of the blest.
On her bosom the poor and oppressed shall recline,
With ennobling surroundings to raise and refine,
While the mothers dread tales to their children will tell
Of an age when was licensed a pathway to hell.

SHIPWRECKED AND SAVED.

Children of earth! who live enthralled
   By that dread tyrant's chain
Whom heathen bards have worshipped
   In many a wild refrain—
Around whose wand'ring, wayward path
   No beams celestial shine,
Your fate enchains my sympathy—
   That gloomy fate was mine.
Break the foul tie that binds the soul,
   Defy the monster's frown,
And when the wine-cup's offered you,
   Indignant dash it down!

I chased the car of Juggernaut,
   A votary in its train,
Regardless of the hecatombs
   Of victims it had slain.
At times a sacrifice aloft
   Upon its arms I hung,

And showered my garlands on the crowd
  While loud their plaudits rung.
I hid the agony endured,
  I shouted back again;
But ever knew and ever felt
  The captive's galling chain.

I chased the *ignis fatuus*
  To many a fatal den,
The fit abode for vampyres—
  God never made for men.
And first to join the revel
  And last to leave the hall,
Amid the bacchanalian songs
  My voice could most enthrall.
But when the boisterous revelry
  Had palled upon my mind,
I saw its hollow vanity,
  I sighed for joys refined.

Sometimes, upon Life's ocean
  My prosperous bark would sail,
And I thought to shun the tempest
  And avoid the driving gale;
But ever when the skies to me

Appeared the most serene,
Dark clouds would round me gather,
Dense mists would intervene.
Sometimes, when gentle zephyrs blew,
I thought the storm to flee;
The next, I, helmless, hopeless drove
Upon Life's stormy sea.

Then Fortune's smile I courted not,
Defied the frowns of fate.
Friendship could not my course avert,
No love, nor scorn, nor hate.
My chart destroyed, my compass broke.
I sped before the blast,
I knew not—I cared not to know—
What land-marks I had passed.
At times an island, fresh and green,
Relieved the scene so dark;
But still I could no refuge find,
No haven for my bark.

In wild profusion then I sowed
The wind upon my path,
And reaped the fatal whirlwind
In its terror and its wrath!

Often the demons I conjured
   Appeared at midnight's hour,
And Horror o'er my senses cast
   Its mystic, mighty power.
Gone were the hopes of former years,
   Forgotten and unknown;
And dead to love, and dead to hate,
   I fought the world alone.

But there are moments in this life,
   By nature's goodness given,
Which, heeded, cause our wond'ring eyes
   To catch some glimpse of heaven.
I heard a voice, as zephyrs mild,
   When summer moon-beams play,
In gentle tones, low-voiced and sweet,
   Say " Shun the tempter's way."
A halo bright was o'er me cast,
   I to the words gave heed;
An angel slumbering woke to life,
   I sprang from thraldom freed.

And 'midst the future scenes of life
   I 'll not forget the hour
When gentle words, in accents mild,

Broke the fell tempter's power.
That moment shall my era be,
 And from that time I'll date,
When, like our Savior on the sea
 You bade the storm abate.
And when upon my heart I wear
 The white, the red, the blue,
Nearer my heart, and still more dear,
 I'll wear my love to you.

Oh, woman! potent is thy spell
 On earth to curse or bless;
Fearful the misery you may cause,
 Supreme the happiness.
Perchance you have no power to bind
 The heartless and the cold,
But you may lead with silken cords
 Th' impulsive and the bold.
On life's forlorn and dreary waste,
 Sweet flow'ret of the glen,
Fulfill your mission, guide and guard
 The steps of wayward men.

SAN QUENTIN'S GRAVES.

'T is the Californian autumn, and the south wind's gentle
    breath
Harbingers the winter's coming and the year's approach-
    ing death.

Misty are the mountain ranges, tawny are the barren hills,
Faded is the summer's verdure, dried the spring-time's
    gushing rills.

And the lesson borne in whispers o'er the zephyr-rippled
    bay
Is the oft-repeated warning—" Passing, passing all away."

Near my feet the mimic billows break around in tiny
    waves,
While behind me, in the shadows, lie San Quentin's out-
    cast graves.

As the evening shadows lengthen, not a sound is faintly
   heard
Save the rustling of some leaflet by the night-wind
   slightly stirred.

Gold is fading into orange in the burnished western skies,
While the Day-God's smile still lingers round the crest of
   Tamalpais.

Scattered glints of shine and shadow softly on the waters
   rest,
Lighting up the fishers' shallops, as in gala vestments
   drest.

While the fading sunlight lingers round thy crest, old
   Tamalpais,
Limning shapes with magic fingers, tell the visions as
   they rise.

You who saw the shadows vanish at creation's dawning
   day,
First to see the Sun-God's arrows light the waters of the
   bay—

When the valley cereal-laden was a mimic inland sea,
Ere the Golden Gate was open, and the imprisoned waters
    free—

Tell us of the ancient Tammals,* who of yore around
    thee roved—
Dusky youths and tawny maidens—how they lived and
    how they loved.

Then rehearse the later story, all the wondrous tale relate,
How the Argonautic Legion sailed into the Golden Gate.

When the fleets of all the nations hither on the billows
    rolled,
To build up the new creations in the real Land of Gold.

Spirit of the Mountain, tell us, you, who nightly vigil
    keep,
Are these restful in their slumbers, happy in their silent
    sleep?

*"Tamalpais" is evidently an idiomatic or mixed word. There
is considerable difference of opinion concerning its derivation.
Pais is "country" in Spanish, and *Tammal* is supposed to be the
name of the tribe of aborigines who lived in what is now Marin
County. Hence, *Tamalpais*—"Country of the Tammals."

Did these never have a mother?—have no gentle sister fair?
Were they always waifs forsaken?—alien to both love and
  care?

Not a flowret blooms above them, not a violet shows its
  face,
Saying, "Mortal, tread more lightly, these were also of
  your race."

Speak! O, Spirit of the Mountain! You who saw their
  grief and fears,
Are these past the pale of mercy who are past the vale
  of tears?

Spake the Mountain—this the answer: "All the past to
  men is dead;
Go! redeem the living present, in the present where you
  tread

"Yonder, near St. Francis City, queenly Mistress of the
  Bay,
Stands Lone Mountain, proud and stately, where the rich
  and honored lie.

"There are tombs, proud mausoleums, spires and statues
    tow'ring high,
Dainty in their sculptured beauty, which are but a sculp-
    tured lie.

"Telling to the humble mourner who shall seek the lonely
    spot,
Not the tenant's life-relations, but precisely what was not.

"Vain are all the towers and columns raised to conquer-
    ors by slaves ;
These are just as near their Maker in San Quentin's out-
    cast graves."

SAN QUENTIN, 1874.

NOTE.—The California State Prison is situated at Point San
Quentin, under the shadow of Mount Tamalpais, the "Monarch of
the Coast Range." In the vicinity is the convicts' burial ground, on
an exposed situation, facing the prevailing winds. Its desolation is
saddening. When we reflect on the fallibility of humanity, and the
hundreds who suffer innocently, and of those who have expiated
their crimes with their end, and the loving hearts which are loyal in
shine and storm, we are ashamed of the civilization which pursues
the unfortunate even after death. There are some who are guiltless.
At the time I speak of, I was an officer at the prison, and have occa-
sion to know something of the subject. I noticed that while the
graves were unmarked, the soil in some places taken away to make
bricks, the cattle roving at will, and no fence, the Chinese had
removed the bones of their countrymen from the desolation.

CHRISTIANITY versus PAGANISM.

1862.

Men of action, men of spirit,
　　Men of power and purpose high,
Ye who love your country's honor,
　　Let no falsehood blind your eye.
From the realm of death and darkness,
　　See advance the pagan band,
Bringing seeds of sure destruction
　　To our fair and happy land.

See the tide of evil swelling,
　　See the desolating blight,
Soon to shroud in gloom eternal
　　Every form of beauty bright;
Spreading base contamination,
　　Foul disease, and moral death,
Worse than earthquake, flood, or famine,
　　Or contagion's blasting breath.

What avails our noble birth-right?
    What avail our fertile plains?
What avails our wealth in treasure?
    What are all our present gains?
If succeeding generations,
    Crushed this cloud of crime beneath,
Curse with bitter imprecations
    We who sow the dragon's teeth.

Let no false or vain delusion
    Of their harmlessness deceive;
❋ Histories of the Mongol Tartar
    No such records ever leave.
Ninety thousand heads of Christians
    Crowned imperial Bagdad's gate,
When Timour, the conquering Pagan,
    Scoured the Syrian land in state.

In the vales of ancient Georgia
    Christian blood in rivers ran;
Demons murdered Christian mothers,
    Fiends, who bore the shape of man.
At the mouths of gloomy caverns,
    Where the Christian fathers fled,
Hung the scaffolds of the scourgers,
    Breathing *hate!* till all were dead.

When Aleppo fell before them,
  And the count of heads was called,
Streamed the streets with blood of maidens,
  While their shrieks the ear appalled!
And at Ispahan a million
  Moslems fell before their stroke;
Spared they neither sex nor station,
  None survived to wear their yoke.

Smyrna fell in glorious conflict
  With the furious Tartar hordes;
Though defended by the valor
  Of the Christian Knights of Rhodes.
From the Volga's icy waters,
  From Damascus to the shore
Of the Ægean Sea, in terror,
  All succumbed to Mongol power!

Still their hatred, unrelenting,
  For the race from which we sprang
Lives! as when from hidden caverns
  Shrieks of Christian Fathers rang.
Stop them not! receive their millions!
  And our race may see again
Desolated homes and hearthstones,
  With the babes and mothers slain!

Curses rest upon the recreants
  Who the slaves of Pagans shield,
To compete with Freedom's labor
  In the workshop and the field!
Rest a gloom upon their household,
  Never cheered by holy song,
Who unto our children's children
  Would bequeath this damning wrong.

'T was the glorious elevation
  Of a labor grand and free,
Ever made our banner worshipped
  Over every land and sea!
For a labor low and servile
  Was the base ambition born,
That *once* sought to make that banner
  In the tyrant's eyes a scorn!

Lessons of material grandeur,
  Taught in every age and clime,
Come to us, as warning beacons,
  Down the misty aisles of time!
Crumbling columns, ruined temples,
  Mouldering, mildew, dust, and blight,
Ancient glory based on serfdom,
  Buried in eternal night.

Surest of all truths, supernal!
 Surer than all man can know,
Are the words of God Eternal,
 "Ye shall harvest what ye sow."
Lofty mountains, stately forests;
 Boundless wealth in vale and glen,
Never can a land ennoble
 Without nobleness in men.

Listen, all ye guides to mortals,
 Ye evangels of the cross!
Ye who preach the blessed Savior,
 Count the gain! and count the loss!
For one angel sent to offer
 Ransom through Messiah's blood,
Pagans come in serried thousands
 To deride the Christian's God!

Better send to ancient Syria,
 And raise Moloch from the grave,
Place him on the desk before you,
 Preaching Christ who died to save;
Search the charnals of the ancients,
 And bring Ashtaroth again!
Bind him to the sacred image,
 While you plead for Jesus slain!

Now let every Freedom-lover
  On this Coast, in every State,
From and past the grand Sierra
  To the ocean's Golden-gate!
Sound the cry! the people's slogan,
  Say "We must—we will—be free
From the desolating scourges
  Of the Asiatic sea!"

Not by vain and useless vaunting,
  Not by threat'nings fierce and wild;
Not by sophistry or canting
  Can we save fair Freedom's child.
Not for base, ignoble trading
  Should our honor be laid low;
Shall they come?—the people's answer
  Must be one eternal "No!"

Human hands frame constitutions;
  Men, not gods, our laws create;
Far outstripping human foresight
  Swelled this tide into our "Gate."
While we hold our father's honor
  Spotless—free from blot or stain,
Like the Macedonian monarch—
  Cleave *this* Gordian knot in twain.

THE DOOM OF THE CUMBERLAND.

Boast ye of courage rare
Where all the fight is fair?
Where grim death's ghastly stare
    May not appal?
Where mid the storm of strife,
Cheered by the drum and fife,
Nerved for the death or life,
    Warriors fall?

There in the fight of chance,
Armed with the sword or lance,
Strong arm and steady glance
    Victory wins.
Faced to the armed foe,
Where ball nor shell can go,
Shielded above, below,
    Courage begins.

On the unruffled bay
We at our anchors lay,
Waiting the close of day,
　　Watching the strife.
Tars of Columbia we,
Sons of the open sea,
Sons of the brave and free,
　　Careless of life.

When came the evening's gloom
Then came the cannon's boom,
Like the dread knell of doom
　　Still drawing near.
But every eye was bright,
And every heart was light,
Nerved for unequal fight,
　　None knew a fear.

Crash! came the hissing shell
O'er the calm waters' swell,
Like some fiend sent from hell
　　Laden with death.
Boldly we took our stand,
Fired at the stern command,
Cheered for our flag and land
　　With the last breath.

Heard we the shot rebound
Through the dense smoke around,
Knew by their hollow sound
    Harmless they were.
Still our fierce battle cry:
" Fighting we live or die,
Never from traitors fly,"
    Rang through the air.

Veered then the monster's prow,
Through us like mist to plow,
Steel yourselves, heroes now,
    Stand to the stroke.
Strong as the whirlwind's might,
Swift as the eagle's flight,
Broke she with demon spite
    Our ribs of oak.

Down through the seething foam,
One thought of friends and home,
Upward our glances roam—
    Shouting we see
Floating serene and bright,
O'er our fast blinding sight—
Wave thou still o'er the fight—
    Flag of the free.

Leuctra nor Marathon,
Nor he of Macedon,
In all the ages gone
Ever hath shown
Courage that dared to do,
What was there done for you,
Flag of our Union true,
" Many in one."

NEVADA CITY, 1862.

6*

THE AMERICAN MOTHER.

'T was when Freedom's cohorts breasted Treason's Cobra
    as its crested
Head was raised to strike the nation for the death or for
    the life,
That a mother, worn and weary, sat throughout the long
    day dreary,
Thinking of her child in battle, on the field of blood and
    strife.
Still was all the scene around her, still as though the
    grief that found her
Thinking of her absent soldier to the very air was known ;
When there came a fatal letter, chaining hope with sor-
    row's fetter :
"Wounded ! Failing "! God of heaven ! is he dying
    there alone ?
Swiftly from her friends she parted ; nothing spake, but
    only started,
And toward her only treasure on the Steam-King's wing
    she flew ;

Short the time until it found her with but stranger faces
round her,

By her youthful soldier's pallet, while his brow was wet
with dew.

As the lengthening of the shadows in the lowlands and
the meadows

Showed the Sun-God was declining in the swiftly dying
day,

Deeper grew the ashy paling on the cheek where life was
failing,

While the Spirits seemed to whisper, " Hold him not, he
may not stay " !

There's a love, a perfect ocean, in a mother's deep devotion—

Not among the loves of mortals can there be a love like
this—

Strong men wept at the beholding of a mother's arms
enfolding

Him unto her beating bosom, for the last, last dying kiss.

Then all earthly comfort scorning, sat she by her dead
till morning—

Till Aurora, from the shadows, ushered in the autumn
morn :

Then without one sign of sadness, but with one sweet
smile of gladness,

Spake she, saying: " Oh, my Country ! Take my all, my
only born !

1863.

THE GRIZZLY TRAP:

AN ADVENTURE IN PLUMAS COUNTY.

It was in the bleak December,
   Eighteen hundred fifty-four,
That I left fair Plumas City,
   Barnard's Diggings to explore.

And I had a comrade with me;
   An old sailor, too, was he—
One whose life had been adventure
   Upon every land and sea.

And he boasted being a Briton,
   And one of that sturdy class
Who were sure to know beforehand
   Everything that came to pass.

We had prospected till evening,
   And the night was drawing near,
When my friend suggested strongly
   We had better homeward steer.

But I knew a storm was rising;
   I could feel it in the breeze,
Hear it in the miserere
   Wailing through the forest trees.

As the trail was blind, untrodden,
   In the daylight but a mark,
I had fear that we could never
   Thread its mazes in the dark.

He was scienced in the woodcraft,
   And my doubt was no avail;
For he knew a shorter cut-off—
   Yes; he knew a plainer trail.

"He would not back out for trifles.
   I was timid well he knew.
Why, the way was plain as preaching.
   He was bound to 'put her through.'"

So we started as the twilight
　　Joined the daylight at its close,
And the wind was blowing stronger,
　　And the falling raindrops froze.

Struggling on in gloomy silence,
　　For 't was plain unto my view
That the path we then were treading
　　Was uncomfortably new.

Till at length I broke the silence
　　And I made this sudden hail:
" Come! I say now, Jack, old fellow,
　　Do you often come this trail?"

" Yes," he answered, " always come it;
　　I know every step I go;
And I know you 'd die this minute
　　If you couldn't make a row."

Then I said: " Heave to a moment;
　　Come and sit down on this log:
This is worse than England-drizzle,
　　Or old Scotia's blinding fog."

"Just like you to be a-growling
  At old England here to-night;
In your bloody mustang country,
  Spitting out your Yankee spite."

But he groped his way toward me,
  And I had not twice to ask,
For I had upon the outset
  Taken the congenial flask.

So we passed a new throat-seizing,
  Rove a lanyard fresh and new,
Hauled well taught the weather-braces,
  And prepared "to put her through."

Filled away among the bushes:
  But 't was very plain to me,
We were sailing in a circle,
  Like a cyclone on the sea.

Soon I hailed him: "Jack, old fellow,
  How 's she heading?   Keep her near;
Seems to me you 're getting sleepy,
  Judging by the way you steer."

Then again he answered, cursing:
  "Yes, I know you 'd raise a row;
Why, the cruise is plain as preaching,
  I know every foot I go."

Then, as if by magic rising,
  Something stood upon the trail,
And again to Jack I shouted—
  Thus I made a welcome hail:

"Steer this way, now, blast your timbers!
  Hard to starboard! never fear;
Who 's the pilot now, old fellow?
  I have made a harbor here."

'T was a cabin, and we entered,
  For we found an open door;
'T was a fire-place that was wanted,
  And for that we did explore.

When there came a sudden tremble,
  Then a most tremendous crash;
Just as something filled the door-way
  Seeming all the place to smash.

Then I said: "Now, Jack, old fellow,
   Did you foreknow this mishap?
Is it not as plain as preaching
   We are in a grizzly trap?"

"Yes," he answered—"always knew it!
   If I did n't, strike me dead;
But I knew it most uncommon
   When I struck that ox's head."

Then I said: "My noble Briton,
   I don't care a single pin;
We are safe for winter quarters,
   And the grizzly 'can't come in.'"

For 't was of the largest timber
   They had made the fatal den;
What would hold the giant monster
   Plainly was too much for men.

In the morning came the miners,
   And they soon were made aware
That the trap had done for Bruin—
   Caught the giant grizzly bear!

Cautiously they gathered round it,
  Anxiously they peered to see
If the trap was any weakened
  By his struggles to be free.

Till one, desperate and daring
  Looked within, and then he stood
Gazing on his friends in wonder,
  For to ice had turned his blood.

"Boys," he said, "this is no grizzly."
  " What the devil is it, then?"
"Boys, as sure as I'm a Christian,
  This is full of living men"!

And they then with heavy levers
  Lifted up the pond'rous door,
And beheld to light emerging
  Two uncommon grizzlies hoar.

Peal on peal of merry laughter
  Through the forest arches rang;
We should have a glorious welcome—
  Be the guests of all the gang.

Soon 't was known around the camp-fires
  How the boys had had a scare;
In their trap had caught two grizzlies—
  Sailor Jack and old Cap. Ware.

Fortune for a time did favor,
  All their knowledge then they told;
Showed us twenty-dollar diggings
  Rich in yellow shining gold.

And my name was ever "Grizzly"
  While I staid around the place;
And I wore my laurels proudly,
  Thinking it was no disgrace.

Sometimes, when the noble Briton
  Strung his long-bow tales to tell,
I would ask him: "Jack, why don't you
  Tell them of the grizzly sell?"

"No, sir! Never! Can't do justice;
  I shall leave that tale for you;
For I never make a practice
  To tell anything that's true."

LA PORTE, PLUMAS COUNTY, 1856.

KINGCRAFT.

———

Who but the blinded dreamer, to whom no truth is plain,
Can harbor the delusion that kingcraft's on the wane?
That men are more republican because of simple form,
Or that forms were ever potent to stay the vengeful
    storm?
Abuses are engendering throughout the land to-day.
No! Forms were never potent to men or nations stay;
And kingcraft is not waning—we know there's no such
    thing,
While here, in free America, monopoly is king.

The reign of kingcraft waning? The sentiment is vain.
What signs of waning kingcraft have risen o'er the slain
In Freedom's last great battle? Go, ask the millionaire,
In sybaritic lodgings, who breathes in perfumed air;
The oily politician, who holds a grand domain
Greater than feudal baron held in kingcraft's darkest
    reign;

Go ask the base contractors who slavish pagans bring
To curse enlightened labor—then boast we have no king.

The reign of kingcraft waning?　When Senators are
　　sold,
Bought by the people's enemies, elected by their gold?
The reign of kingcraft waning?　When those who crept
　　before,
Raised by the people's ballot, assert the kingly power
To lord it o'er their masters, and, insolent as fate,
Say—boldly say—"Bow down to us and worship : we're
　　the State."
No; kingcraft is not waning, nor the misery it brings,
While, railing against kingcraft, we bow to scores of
　　kings.

The first is King Monopoly—the power behind the
　　throne.
The next is smooth-tongued Policy, which seeks for self
　　alone.
The next is King Expediency, who never values "right,"
And Insincerity we have—a mildew, curse, and blight;
And many more ignoble kings, whom here we dare not
　　name ;
And Falsehood, leading king of Hell, may here an empire
　　claim.

What power can save the nation's life? What can avert
   our fate
While all these kings hold carnival within the halls of
   State?

The reign of kingcraft waning? When monarchs seek
   our shore
The men bow down in homage, the women all adore;
The children are brought out to see the thing they call
   divine,
And see the stars and garters and tinsel on him shine.
"Beware," said grand old Washington, "of kingly forms
   beware—
To principles republican a lure, a curse, a snare."
And still the people crowd the street, and silent homage
   bring,
While saying kingcraft's waning, to see a living king.*

The heathen makes his idol in the far pagan lands,
Then bows in reverence before the work of his own hands;
But if the worshipped idol betrays his humble trust,
'T is hurled from its pedestal—kicked, buried in the dust.
We Christians too make idols; and when the gods deceive,
We bow in humble homage — 't is ours, not theirs, to
   grieve.

*Kalakaua, the King of the Cannibal Islands.

We cringe before the thing we made, and abject fealty
    bring,
And keep the gods we raise in power, and rail against a
    king.

Come forth, ye sons of labor! and stop the threatened
    doom,
Let the farmer leave the furrow—the weaver leave the
    loom;
Let the smith upon his anvil a mighty chorus sound,
With sparks from freedom's hammer make all enchanted
    ground—
Till from the ranks of labor, defiant, bold, and free,
We raise anew to splendor the **Tree of Liberty.**

Come, miner, leave the tunnel, with sweat upon your brow;
To stop these great abuses your country needs you now.
Come, citizens of every class, and boldly take your stand,
You are the latent power which yet shall save fair Free-
    dom's land;
Your cause is just and holy, 'tis not for blood or spoil,
'T is to break down all kingcraft, and honor honest toil.

MY FATHER'S QUARTZ TUNNEL.

When my eyes shall no more see the scenes of my child-
    hood,
  The hills of Nevada my infancy knew,
Its sage-bush and cedars, its mountains and wild-wood,
  The home, my dear mother, made happy by you;
I know that one spot will come back to my vision,
  Though the storms of life's winter my heart-strings may
    chill,
And though rough, 't will appear to my fancy elysian,
  My father's quartz tunnel that pierces the hill;
        The dark, silent tunnel,
        The weird, lonely tunnel,
My father's quartz tunnel that pierces the hill.

How often I stand at its mouth in the cañon,
  And gaze in its depths the dense gloom to explore;
With what weird, mystic shapes, does my fancy compan-
    ion

The caves where my father blasts out the bright ore.
Will I find, in my manhood, a realization
Of what now with wonder my fancy does fill,
As I stand on the track at the end of the station
And gaze in the tunnel that pierces the hill?
   The dark, silent tunnel,
   The weird, lonely tunnel,
My father's quartz tunnel that pierces the hill.

Sometimes at the mouth of the tunnel I listen,
 And hear wond'rous tales from the men of the mine,
Of the old "Pioneers," and I see their eyes glisten,
 Rehearsing the glories of famed Forty-nine.
More wond'rous than those of old Sinbad, the sailor,
 Or of Jack, who went forth the great Giant to kill,
Or the Argonaut maiden with none to bewail her,
 Are the tales of the tunnel that pierces the hill;
   The cold, silent tunnel,
   • The weird, mystic tunnel,
My father's quartz tunnel that pierces the hill.

All over the mountains, and down on the river,
 Throughout our young State there are tunnels, I 'm
  told,
Where brave hearts and strong arms still work to deliver

7

The mountains of treasure in silver and gold.
And there's many like me in the mountains and wild-
    wood,
Whose hearts in the future with pleasure will thrill,
As they think of some wild, wond'rous scene of their
    childhood,
  Some dark, silent tunnel away on the hill;
        Some dark, mystic tunnel,
        Some moss-covered tunnel,
  Some rock-caverned tunnel away on the hill.

WHO FOLLOWETH THE WINE-CUP CAN NEVER EXCEL.

Yes! dash down the wine-cup! the tempter destroy,
The life of your sorrow, the death of your joy;
Thirty centuries now have passed over the earth
Since these words from Divine Inspiration had birth.
In all ages succeeding their truth has been shown,
For the wisest of earth let the wine-cup alone.
Let it sound in your ears like a death-tolling knell,
" He who followeth the wine-cup can never excel."

He may know every nation, and talk every tongue
Ever sage has expounded or ministrel has sung
From the cold frozen North, with its winters of gloom,
To the land of the Tropics whose flowers ever bloom ;
Though his wit may enliven, his lore may inform
Of bright sunny regions, or whirlwind and storm,
And tell all the dooms that have nations befell—
Still " who followeth the wine-cup can never excel."

Though he hath every power that to mortals is given
By Nature's bequest, or the goodness of heaven,
And still the one passion he cannot restrain,
A captive, he goes but the length of his chain.
If powers most transcendent are trod in the earth,
'T were better, far better, he never had birth;
With a hold upon Heaven, he still chooses Hell,
For " who followeth the wine-cup can never excel."

Though his brow may impress, and his eye may inspire
Deep trust in its power, by electrical fire;
Like Prometheus of old, he is chained to the rock,
And endures without shelter the elements' shock:
While deep on his vitals the vulture still feeds,
And powerless, and stricken, his torn bosom bleeds;
And he there without hope, without mercy, must dwell,
For " who followeth the wine-cup can never excel."

Though his eloquence, god-like, enthralls and enchains,
And reverence and love from the multitude gains,
As unmasking deceit, or expounding the law,
He holds all around in deep silence and awe;
Though the thrill of his voice and the light of his eye
May inspire lofty purpose, pure, holy, and high;
Example enforces no truths he can tell,
For " who followeth the wine-cup can never excel."

The greatest of conquerors the world has yet known,
Who for years kept all nations in fear of his frown,
Whom nor mountains, nor rivers, could stop on his way,
When he marshalled his armies to ravage and slay,
Succumbed to the wine-cup, drooped, lingered, and died
In the pride of his manhood, the zenith of pride;
With schemes half accomplished, a victim he fell,
For " who followeth the wine-cup can never excel."

THE TAINT IS IN MY BLOOD.

It was a curious letter, with sacred scenes to blend;
It came at a peculiar time—'t was Christmas tide, my
    friend:
We'll try to solve the mystery and see where it will end.

Amid much that might encourage there was more that
    might depress—
A tribute unto vanity, but nothing that could bless
The giver or receiver; and though I cast away
The letter most contemptuously, the sentiment would
    stay.
And I have pondered over its meaning many an hour,
And asked myself the question: "Is there on earth a
    power—
A curse—entailed, inherited, by nature understood?
And is the writer's judgment true—"The taint is in
    your blood."

It spake of grand possessions, inheritance of mind,
Ennobled aspirations, and sentiments refined;

Of insight into deeper things, of power but seldom given

To almost grasp the infinite and read the thoughts of
heaven ;

Of treasures of intelligence, lost, squandered, cast away;

Of darkness where there should be light, of night where
should be day ;

And hinted, more than hinted, I had been false to
God—

One curse had swallowed all of good—"The taint was in
my blood."

'T was strange, for unseen messengers did walk with me
that day,

And said: "Beware perdition's path, and go where
Christians pray."

And I had sought a temple, endowed with costly care,

Where the grand organ's notes I heard in cadences most
rare ;

But o'er the grand orchestral notes, the dimly softened
sheen,.

The painted frescoes, angel-typed, the weird, bewildering
scene,

Above the emblemed evergreens, the painted windows'
light,

I heard the old, old anthem sung of that eventful night

When first it struck the shepherds' ears, I heard the chant
    again :
" Glory to God ! the highest, give ; on earth, good will to
    men."

Again my mental vision gazed, and spirit eyes did see
The Saviour preaching to the poor of old, on Galilee ;
Next saw the cross on Calvary's Mount and heard the
    jeering crew—
Now, Notre Dame des Victoires, I bow to Christ and you.
I left the church, I sought again the revel on the street ;
But not among the thousands there one thoughtful face
    did meet ;
Among the superficial throng, the city's sensuous flood
I stood alone ! there was not one who thought of Christ
    as God—
So when the letter me condemned for loss of fame or
    pelf,
I thought of Him of whom 't was said : " He cannot save
    himself."
The mists of nineteen hundred years passed by. I saw
    his grave—
I saw the meek-browed watchers there who dared all
    scorn to brave,
And over all I heard the taunt : " Himself he cannot save."

The black flag floats at my mast-head, there placed by
    Nature's God ;
I cannot, if I would be saved—"The taint is in my blood."

Again I wandered down the street, the mystery to un-
    fold—
The day had passed, the ocean wind was damp and
    deadly cold—
From many a palace haunt of sin, and down in dark-
    some hells,
Where moral pestilence prevails and base contagion
    dwells,
The sounds of revel broke upon the stillness of the night.
The Saviour's natal day was cursed, to sow the seeds of
    blight;
For if the writer's judgment's true, if thus the seed is
    sown,
I, in the coming century, could never stand alone;
The lost will count by millions, for raging is the flood
That bears this fatal sum of mine—"the taint that's in
    my blood."

SAN FRANCISCO, DEC. 25TH, 1874.

7*

THE REIGN OF TEMPERANCE:

OR

THE ANGEL'S MISSION.

'T is Winter! and fierce reigns the Storm king without,
And the demons that gather are darkness and doubt,
And I ask from Omniscience, who rides on the gale,
Shall these evil surroundings forever prevail?
Shall the demon who rides on the wings of the wind,
And whose track leaves despair and destruction behind,
Be permitted to triumph, still triumph o'er man,
To defeat thy decrees, thy beneficent plan?
See! an Angel appears, and a message she brings,
And 't is thus the fair Angel enchantingly sings:

"I have come, lily-robed, in my mantle of white,
   All discord and strife to destroy.
I an olive-branch bear, from the region of light,
   Where love only my subjects employ.

I have come, lily-robed, in my mantle of white,
   To my own, to my chosen domain;
To the soil where the ashes of martyrs repose,
   Who to hasten my mission were slain;
Where, effulgent, the fair tree of liberty grows,
   I have come to renew my lost reign;
And though glorious the song that the morning-star sang,
   I now hear a more blissful refrain,
As from mountains and valley, from forest and glade,
   From lakelet and river and sea,
I now hear the glad voice of a people redeemed,
   From the Wine-Fiend's dominion set free.
And I know the glad shout that arises and swells
From the mountain's high crest to the mine's deepest cells
   Is a world-given welcome to me.
To me! as I come in my mantle of white,
From my home in the Cloud-Land, resplendently bright,
   Lily-robed to the World's Jubilee."

MORTAL.

" And art thou, fair Angel, a Princess of Peace?
   A Princess of Salem's blest line?
Hast thou come claiming kindred and faith in the star
   That of yore did o'er Bethlehem shine?
To restore its lost glory, oh, Princess serene,
And the reign of its kingdom benign?"

" Yes : I am the Angel, long sorrowing and sad,
   Who hath watched through the ages in vain
For some redeemed spot on the lost earth to rest,
   And to hear the glad anthem again
Which was sang at creation, and echoed in love
   To the shepherds on Chaldea's plain ;
So I pierced the cloud realm of the earth in my flight,
To discover the cause of its darkness and blight.

" First I lighted in a palace where the fiend in golden
    chalice
Holds dominion o'er the mortals men style emperors and
    kings,
And I saw amid their revels the one power that greatness
    levels
To the lowness of the reptiles that are called instinctive
    things ;
Saw beneath their robes of splendor, there the ignoble
    surrender
Of the dowry of immortals, of the heritage divine ;
Saw each lofty aspiration that attends the soul's salvation
Basely squandered ! vilely bartered ! for the groveling of
    the swine ;

Saw the sycophantic minions onward borne upon the
pinions
Of the fiend, to deeper darkness than the poor can ever
know;
And I thought as silent gazing on a horror so amazing,
These are scarcely worth the saving from the clutches of
the foe.
So I turned me from the portals of the great among the
mortals,
For I thought the angel Mercy had forever closed the
door;
That their lamp, but dimly lighted, had gone out, forever
blighted,
Past the power of man or angel in the future to restore.
West I turned, and crossed the ocean, where in freedom's
deep devotion
Men decreed that royal baubles all were vain and sense-
less things;
Had denied their divination, and attendant pomp and
station,
And professed to worship only the Eternal King of
Kings.
In their halls of legislature, where but men of mental
stature
Should be chosen as the guardians of the millions of the
free!

There I stood and gazed in wonder, that a stroke of God's
    own thunder
Did not strike the desecrators who revere all gods but He.
There the Wine-King held his ruling in bravado or in
    puling,
Never higher than the ceiling did an aspiration soar;
Never farther than the present could the solons, evanes-
    cent,
Frame a purpose or a measure to the lost of earth re-
    store;
Still the Wine-Fiend held dominion, and his cry was
    always 'More.'
Sad I left, and sought a hovel where the poor in squalor
    grovel,
Where God's own, and Christ's anointed, on the earth
    are doomed to stay;
There I heard a supplication, in itself an expiation,
From a lone and widowed mother for her erring son
    astray,
From a broken hearted mother for her drunken son
    astray.
Almost famished, past the striving, still the mother's love
    surviving,
Ever living, all prevailing, prayed she thus to God above:
'God of mercy! God of justice! In whose love our only
    trust is,

Why should woman bear the burden, for the sins of those
    they love ?
Be deceived in life's fair morning, made the idle jest and
    scorning
Of the drunkard's frenzied fury, of the drunkard's sense-
    less mirth.
Well we know, a cause redeeming, if 't were only right
    in seeming,
That would stop the monster's ravage, drive the demon
    from the earth.
Thou, of worlds the great Creator! *Thou*, of destiny
    dictator,
Give to woman power for action, and from right she 'll
    never swerve.
Till the alcoholic demon finds a fate he does not dream
    on,
Fate of swift and sure destruction, which both God and
    man will serve.' "

Then there came a revelation, heralding a new salvation,
As from out the night and darkness, spake the voice di-
    vine and said :
" Woman ! soon his reign is ending, from this time in pur-
    pose blending,
You with man shall act in concert, till the tyrant scourge
    has fled."

MORTAL.

" Now, what is the vision, oh, Angel of light,
　　You behold from your home in the skies?
　Is the swift-coming future resplendent and bright?
　　Shall your star to the zenith arise? "

ANGEL.

" Yes! the swift-coming future before me is read,
And the obsolete issues of mortals are dead;
For the God of Omniscience, who governs the gale,
Hath decreed that good over the ill shall prevail,
And that Man having failed 'gainst the fiend in despair,
Hath at length implored Woman the burden to share;
Not the burden of sorrow, or burden of grief,
But the burden of ' rule ' for a nation's relief;
And she, proudly conscious in right of the dower,
Brings against the fell fury the force of her power;
And no longer confined to beseeching and prayer,
With the ' ballot ' has ended the reign of despair."

MORTAL.

" Still longer, fair Angel : we ask you to tell,
　After Woman had conquered on earth, what befell?"

ANGEL.

" Now the spring time has come, and the zephyrs of May
From the widow's lone cottage drive winter away,
While home has returned the lost child that was gone,
And reclines on her heart like the prodigal son ;
For the mother who prayed on the promise reclines
Of Him who the secrets of mortals divines,
And the children's glad shouts ringing forth in their glee
Show that they from the mighty destroyer are free."

MORTAL.

" Once more, oh ! fair Angel: we ask you again,
On the earth what befell ere the end of her reign ?"

ANGEL.

" Oh ! favored of earth; now the visions of old
    Find a realization for you ;
Your mountains yield silver, your rivers run gold,
    And your harvests yield plenty as dew.

" O'er the bleak, barren plain, strewn with bones of the
    slain,

Proud, defiant, the steam whistle blows;
Rough places are smoothed, crooked paths are made
    straight,
  And the wilderness blooms as the rose.
Now rejoice in your pride, for your fame is world-wide—
  Let the name of my kingdom resound;
Your escutcheon so bright is emblazoned in light,
  Since this last fetter fell to the ground.
I now see your advance, it is clear to my glance,
  And 't is bathed in a halo of light,   .
Since I came to the earth from the place of my birth,
  Lily-robed in my mantle of white.
The oppressed from afar shall behold the new star,
  And with longing shall seek its embrace,
And the fame of your land through the ages shall stand,
  While the smile of God rests on its face;
For Woman has conquered the fiend, and retrieved
  The loss of that Eden for which the world grieved;
And redeemed past the power of his lure to beguile,
  She may challenge the sunlight to rival her smile."

'T is finished! 't is finished! the message she brings,
And 't is thus the fair Angel enchantingly sings.

TRAMPS.

"LOOK ON THAT PICTURE, AND ON THIS."

In his Eastern home midst plenty,
   In the grand old Buckeye State,
With his wife and children round him,
   Scorned he all the frowns of fate.
Plenty smiled around his threshold,
   And no wolf was at his door;
Why has he become a vagrant,
   And a Tramp from shore to shore?

Shall I tell you?   Will you listen?
   'T was the base and treacherous clan,
False to country, god, and duty,
   Who delude their fellow man;
Paid by aliens' corporations,
   San Francisco's lying sheet,

Never speaking of the pagans
　　Who, like locusts, swarm the street.

"Oh? the mountains were all silver,
　　And the rivers sown with gold,
Here the vintage wept its nectar
　　Like elysian vales of old.
Here the harvests gleamed in plenty,
　　Roamed the flocks and shed the fleece
That were claimed for old Arcadia's
　　Fabled realm of joy and peace."

So he called his darlings round him,
　　Saying : " In a little time
I shall make a princely fortune
　　In the glorious golden clime."
And since then the man has wandered ;
　　But wherever he may go,
To each question for employment
　　It is one eternal " No."

Curses rest upon the recreants
　　Who abuse the printer's art,
Paid by grasping coalitions
　　To enact the villain's part.

Many a household in the East-land
  Never knew a grief or wail
Till some sycophantic minion
  Told his false delusive tale.

Many a " Tramp " to-day is marching
  To find out some treasure-field ;
Plodders, rot! 't is visionaries
  Always find the precious yield.
Since the Argonautic Legion
  Did of yore to Colchis sail,
" Tramps " explored each mountain fastness—
  Sailed on every ocean's gale.

Tell me! ye who live by miners
  Working in the deadly damps,
Where the sun-light never enters,
  Think you none of them were " Tramps "
Where would be your mountain city,
  Where your wealth in shining ore,
Had the " Tramps " not found the treasure
  Ere you came, in days of yore ?

Beat him ! kick him from the axle !
  How has he a right to ride

Underneath the railroad palace
  Where the Nabobs sit in pride?
Drive him forth into the country—
  Banish him to lonely camps—
But remember, treasure-finders
  Are, and always have been, "Tramps."

THE VOICE OF THE PEOPLE.

What sound strikes the ear since the nation, redeemed,
　　Seemed beyond the dread threat'ning of fate?
What sound has awakened the lovers of right
　　To the perils that threaten the State?
'T is the voice of the People by suffering taught,
　　Each infringement of right to review;
'T is the voice of the People awakened again,
　　By the vigilant, watchful, and true,
Saying: "Children, the heritage saved by our blood
　　Is now squandered, or stolen from you."

Half a century since, in the senate unchained,
　　Did the giant of intellect stand,*
And combatted there despoilers of right
　　Who had lived on the sweat of the land.
There conscious of power, like the Grecian of old,
　　The Modern Demosthenes said:

* "Sir! The People of the North is the North."—*Webster's Reply to Calhoun.*

"We are fighting for issues, fresh, teeming with life!
    You are fighting for issues now dead."
'T is the land! not the people! not the many, the few,
    Represent the green vales of the South.
While the People! the People! reliant and true,
    Represent the bleak hills of the North.
Now the voice of the People, awakened again,
    By the vigilant, watchful, and true,   ·
Says: "Children, the land bought by treasure and blood
    Shall no longer be stolen from you."

Let monopolies thrive, combinations advance,
    Rings, factions, and money-kings reign;
And the blood of the patriots who died to redeem—
    'T was a sacrifice offered in vain.
If allowed in this land, ere a century hence,
    'T will be said as in Britain said now,
By the class who descend from usurpers of rights,
    Not one acre of land shall endow
The descendants of those by whose labor we live,
    The poor slaves of the pick, spade, and plow.
Come forth to the rescue, arise at the call
    Of the vigilant, watchful, and true,
And say: "Children, the land bought by treasure and
    blood,
    Must henceforth be a dowry for you."

VIRTUE'S ITS OWN REWARD.

"He fought his doubts and gathered strength;
He would not make his judgment blind,
He fought the specters of the mind,
And laid them; till at length
He made a stronger faith his own.
And power was with him in the night,
Which makes the darkness and the light,
And dwells not in the light alone."
—[*Tennyson's "In Memoriam."*]

I know that 'midst the axioms old,
  Time's current has brought down
To raise a smile, bring forth a tear,
  Perchance provoke a frown,
There's *one* shall in the future live,
  One Time shall ever guard;
It is the simple axiom that
  "Virtue's its own reward."

In this, the so-called age of light,
  Were all things fairly shown,

It would be seen that virtue hides,
  And vice usurps the throne.
From worldly hopes of preference,
  Virtue appears debarr'd,
Which seems to prove that virtue must
  Be virtue's own reward.

Still, travelers on the word's highway,
  Who toil their journey through,
Who fight for right, because 't is right,
  To conscience ever true,
Shall find a peace no wealth can buy,
  Shall heed no man's regard,
Shall independent live and die:
  "Virtue's its own reward."

There's many a fairy, sylph-like form
  Bedecked with jewels bright,
Which gleam and sparkle in the dance,
  Transfiguring the night,
With voice attuned to love's soft tones,
  By feigned emotions stirred;
Would give her jewels all to know,
  "Virtue's its own reward."

There's many a brain all conscienceless,
   Now striving to be great,
In the vain hope that happiness
   Can never come too late;
Who yet shall find their Angels fair,
   Are Demons bleared and scarred,
Shall learn too late this truth of truths,
  "Virtue's its own reward."

The crowns of monarchs, what are they?
   The courts where pleasure reigns;
The pleasure that beyond the hour,
   No source of bliss maintains;
The glory that the conqueror wins,
   The wealth that misers hoard,
Are bubbles that a breath will break:
  "Virtue's its own reward."

We leave unto the misty past
   Its relics and its creeds.
Perchance when superstition reigned,
   She met the people's needs.
The motto that our emblem bears,
   Is now, was always, true:
"Do not to others what you would
   They should not do to you."

Prepare! The moral conflict comes;
   Do battle for the right;
Renew your faith in virtue's cause,
   The people need your fight.
Though fools may laugh, and fiends may gibe,
   Our banner, many-starred,
Must be upheld by those who think
   " Virtue 's its own reward."

The soul's calm sunshine beams for those
   Who follow virtue's path,
And passion's tempest never hurls
   On such, its storm of wrath.
The Angel Peace, with outstretched wings,
   Holds o'er them heavenly guard,
While in their inner lives they *know*,
   " Virtue 's its own reward."

THE BEAUTIES OF NATURE.

Most beauteous things of Nature are heeded not, if seen—
The heavens' celestial azure, the earth's life-giving green;
The varied change of seasons, the sunshine and the storm;
The winter's bracing breezes, the summer's zephyrs warm;
But the mountain and the valley, and the islands of the
    sea,
Present images of beauty which give pleasure unto me.
And everything in Nature's face for me has something
    fair;
And my eye its beauty mirrors as my lungs inspire its air.
And thus 't was ever with me; for even when a boy,
Amid the winter's howling blast, my heart leaped forth for
    joy,
And each shaded cove and inlet that lay on the river's
    shore,
In the balmy days of summer 't was my pleasure to ex-
    plore,
To watch the varied changes as my boat did gently glide,
Or in the eddying current, or in the rushing tide;

Where sometimes the huge bowlders their hoary crests
 upreared,
With saline grasses covered, like ancient Sea-Kings'
 beard.
My comrades gazed in wonder—a feeling strange to me—
Why oftentimes I floated for many miles to sea;
But they knew not of the mystery which cast o'er me its
 spell,
Nor the beauty I was tracing on the ocean's gentle swell.
In after life I paced the deck in midnight's darkest hour,
And saw the tempest culminate and clouds portentous
 lower;
And even then I beauty saw, as, gazing on the wake,
I saw a myriad bubbles rise, sparkling in light to break.
And even on the tow'ring west the sight would joy in-
 spire,
As I beheld the good ship cleave her way through liquid
 fire.
The iceberg, dreaded of all dreads, was beautiful to me,
Ocean's imperial palace—the cathedral of the sea;
For on its glittering domes I saw a million sparkling rays,
Shaming the studied works of art—giving to Nature praise
Beauty I saw in southern climes, where spikes of coral
 grow,
Red, like the tint on beauty's cheek, or spotless as the
 snow.

Beauty! when first unto the gaze are little islands seen
Emerging from the ocean depths, in emerald hues of
    green.
Beauty! when, on some wooded height, the eye could
    faintly trace
The water-falls, like silver threads, rush down the moun-
    tain face.
Beauty! amid the foliage dense that giant trees entwines,
Presenting to the distant view a pyramid of vines.
There's beauty in the northern land—'t is when the
    tempest hurls
Its storm of sleet, and leaves each tree laden with glist'ning
    pearls;
T'is when the sun's reflected rays upon the ice-trees shine,
A cold and crystal beauty glows nearest on earth divine.
And gems of beauty rich and rare are scattered o'er the
    earth;
There is no spot on Nature's face that gives not beauty
    birth.
But beautiful, more beautiful than *all* these sights and
    scenes—
The mountain's stately forests, the valley's lovely greens;
The mountain's noble grandeurs, the valley's lovely flow-
    ers;
The monotone of sighing winds, the sunshine and the
    showers;

The song-bird's charming melody, the rainbow's glittering
    beam;
The painter's art, the minstrel's song, the poet's glorious
    dream;
The zephyrs of Arcadian isles, whose gardens know no
    storm—
Is beauty, when to virtue joined in woman's beauteous
    form.

"WHAT MIGHT HAVE BEEN."

Midst all the sayings, true or false,
  Brought down by tongue or pen,
There's one has palsied many a hope,
  That contrasts *now* with *then*.
That mourns o'er buried wishes dead,
  And would fresh sorrow glean
From what we were, and what we are,
  And from "What might have been."

I have a friend — a valued friend —
  Whose tears may never dry,
Who often speaks in plaintive tone
  And sad, desponding eye;
And says, "We're nearing now the goal
  Of three-score years and ten,
With none to care; I can but grieve
  O'er that which "might have been."

I said: "My friend, the man who lives
  And retrospects the years,

And scrutinizes others' griefs,
   Their follies, and their fears —
And finds himself in health and strength,
   With conscience pure and clean,
Need never give a single thought
   On that which ' might have been.' "

He said : " If I 'd done this or that,
   Or gone some other way,
I might have had some station great,
   Or wealth or fame, to-day.
The chances I did not-improve
   Are now so clearly seen,
That I must grieve o'er what I am,
   And o'er 'what might have been.' "

I said : " I saw a stately dame
   Arrayed in laces rare,
Who looks upon the ' lower class '
   With supercilious air.
I learned that on her unblessed couch
   By all but God unseen,
She mourns a false and heartless life,
   Grieves o'er 'what might have been.' "

Upon the world's great stage there's some
　　Must play the lower parts,
Who, if they may not diamonds hold,
　　Had better play for hearts;
For could they strip from fashion's pets,
　　The glitter and the sheen,
They'd find that even envied ones,
　　Grieve o'er " what might have been."

The grieving o'er " what might have been "
　　Will not one sorrow heal;
The man who mourns " what might have been "
　　Will not move fortune's wheel.
There's one thing that's so clearly plain
　　The blindest fool must see,
The question's not " What might have been?"
　　It is " What is to be?"

So dry your tears my sorrowing friend,
　　Make this complaint the last;
The disappointments of this life
　　Are o'er when they are past.
'T is God alone has power to know,
　　The great profound unseen;
We know what was—we know what is—
　　There is no " might have been."

So I advise my youthful friends
　　To cultivate the thought,
That nothing's past redemption here,
　　Or *was*, and there is not
To catch that charity that comes
　　From heaven, an unseen power,
That makes another's noxious weed,
　　To ope a beauteous flower.

Let no such thing as *policy*
　　Direct you in life's flight,
For when a thing seems *right* to *you*,
　　Be sure to *you* 't is *right*.
Take conscience only for your guide,
　　As you the world begin,
And right or wrong you'll never grieve
　　O'er that which " might have been."

TO THE MEXICAN VETERANS.

———

The bright May morn broke fair and clear,
   The south-wind's warm caresses
Shimmered the leaves on Carson's trees
   And waved her maidens' tresses.
From arid slopes and valleys green
   The old and young were coming
To decorate the soldiers' graves,
   That balmy spring-time morning.
But quite alone one band there marched,
   Whose hair was tinged with gray;
Like the Old Guard and Tour d'Auvergne,
   They had been in the fray;
For they had fought in Mexico,
   And veterans true were they.
And as I gazed, before me rose
   Brave Taylor's little band,
When first encamped, in Forty-Six,

Beside the Rio Grande.
In fancy then the old-time fight
    I saw fought o'er again.
I passed through "Angostura's Gorge,"
    To Buena Vista's plain;
For I, an "Argonaut," knew well
    Those fights were not in vain.
I heard as though 't were yesterday
    Bold Ringgold's thrilling tone—
"Comrades, go on; your duty calls.
    The brave can die alone."
Heard Taylor say, "Go, take those guns,"
    And Captain May reply,
"I 'll do it, sir, or every man
    In my command will die!"
'T was done; and History is proud
    The noble deed to tell,
And how, deserted by his men,
    The brave La Vega fell.
'T was the commencement of the war,
    And hushed all vain alarms.
The battle-ground in English is
    The "Valley of the Palms."

Through bloody fights and victories won,
    I followed on the way,

But stopped to shed a tribute tear
    For her of Monterey ; *
Who, following mercy's mission there
    Upon the fields of strife,
Was struck by some ill-omened shot,
    And yielded up her life.
Again on Buena Vista's heights
    I saw the battle flag,
And heard Zach Taylor, cursing, say
    " More grape there, Captain Bragg."
And then the panorama changed,
    And grand old Scott appeared,
Brave as a lion, kind and true,
    By all his men revered.
Then Cerro-Gordo's pass uprose,
    And Plan del Rio's green,
While the majestic form of Scott
    Still tower'd above the scene :
And the same veterans I saw
    Who now walk here to-day,
Fight at the mill of some old king
    Called Molino del Rey ;
And though a later war eclipsed

---

*It is said that a Mexican woman, while bringing water to the wounded and dying, friend or foe, was killed by a stray ball at the battle of Monterey. There is a ballad in celebration of the fact, called "The Maid of Monterey."

The grandeur of that time,
The Argonauts will not forget
They won the golden clime.
They scaled the Cordillera's crest,
No loss their valor quenched,
Until upon Ayotla's height
The army stood intrenched;
Around the Lakes of Chalco, then,
And Xochimilico,
I saw these gray-haired veterans march
With stately step and slow;
And though my memory wandered back
To Wolfe and old Quebec,
A grander scene appeared to view
On famed Chapultepec;
For students there fought to the death,
As did the priests of yore,
When Spaniards won the Aztec throne
Three hundred years before,
And Montezuma's halls were won
The throne and diadem.
What wonder that I joined the ranks,
And wished to walk with them?
For well I know this Western Shore—
This grand Pacific strand—
Was won by that immortal few,
Mexico's Veteran Band.

CARSON CITY.

"GO, SIN NO MORE."

He stood, and wrote upon the ground; and as He wrote, He seemed
to ask Himself the question: "Shall I make void the law Levitical,
and brave the fury of the Pharisaic crowd?" Yes; He, the teacher
of a dispensation new, rebuked the grovelling pride which seeks
to build on others' ruin; and thus the Savior spoke: "Neither do I
condemn thee. Go, and sin no more."

Take heart now, O wanderer from virtue's path straying,
   On whom some shadow rests, darkening thy day;
For there's a Comforter, one ever praying
   Heaven to direct you in virtue's blest way.
Perhaps, as in Jesus' time, some, all unheeding,
   May have forgotten that none can be pure,
May have crushed some poor heart, lonely and bleeding,
   Past all the power Heaven gave to endure.
Turn again to the Light from the Fount streaming;
   To the Reproachless One let your thoughts soar;
Day has now dawned for you—see its light beaming!
   The Saviour still says to you, "Go, sin no more."

Heed not the world's scorn, be not forsaken,
   While the Immaculate sorrows for thee;

If your firm faith in Him shall not be shaken,
   You, though a captive long, soon shall be free.
Fond hearts are waiting now, arms are extended
   Again to enfold you in tender embrace;
Rancor has vanished now, hatred has ended,
   They, too, have seen the smile lighting His face.
On the bosom of virtue henceforward reclining,
   And trusting the Holy One all should adore,
New tendrils of love 'round your crushed heart entwining
   Shall prove your forgiveness; then "Go, sin no more."

Come back! O come back! to the home of life's morning,
   For the lilies of purity still there do bloom;
But brighter they'll bloom, with your presence adorning,
   The home which your absence has shrouded in gloom.
Come back! O come back! why, this world's not all winter!
   Even storms, clouds, and darkness some pleasure may
      bring,
By enhancing the beauty, effulgence, and splendor
   Of the verdure that heralds the beautiful spring.
Renew the blest age when your life was all sunshine,
   The happy Elysium you dwelt in of yore;
Since He, the Reproachless, extends his forgiveness,
   And says "I condemn thee not. Go, sin no more."

VIRGINIA CITY, 1867

MUSING BY THE SPRING.

The summer breeze was fresh and sweet that bright
    Nevada day,
When musingly I strolled along to where the garden lay
Just fifteen fleeting years before, in verdure green and
    gay.

No house was there, no garden fair, nor any winsome
    thing
To tell of fairer, brighter scenes, or fresh to memory
    bring
The shout of childhood's happier day—only the sylvan
    spring.

And silently I sat beside the spring and round me gazed,
I knew that years seemed ages here, and still I felt amazed
To see the desolation round, for nature's self seemed
    crazed.

I knew the sagebrush was no rose, the cedar dwarf no
    palm,
I knew the Washoe zephyr blows no gales of fragrant
    balm—
But I had seen oases rare in sweet secluded calm;

Where happy homes 'mid flowrets grew, and children
    prattled round,
And sweet contentment made the spots to me seem hal-
    lowed ground,
Far from the city's vice and strife, with humble plenty
    crowned.

There musingly I pondered o'er the present and the past,
The changes and the chances which life's horoscope had
    cast
On them, while mournfully I asked, "Shall this fate be
    the last."

For there I left young maidenhood, and matron's bloom-
    ing prime,
And merry children full of glee, in their sweet summer
    time,
And manhood, full of purpose too, and courage most sub-
    lime!

Oh Innovation! on your track, and Progress at your call,
Like giants, noxious evils rise, on happy homes to fall;
And though I close my eyes, I see "the rich are all in all."

And while I there on progress thought, a shriek disturbed
 the air,
'T was not the savage warwhoop, 't was for some as near
 despair,
It was the engine's shout, and said: "Make way, my path
 prepare!"

'T is said 't is progress, and 't is said "Its work has just
 begun";
Perhaps! I knew of hamlets fair whose race were quickly
 run,
And some still think it only means "toil many for the
 one."

Yes, build your highway o'er the hills, do all that wealth
 can do,
Pile up your costly palaces, and keep their domes in view;
Advancement! and aggrandisement! yes! for a favored
 few.

The veil is lifted from my eyes, the curtain from my sight,
What men accept as progress now, in future may be
    blight,
If mammon's the republic's God! and might's enthroned
    o'er right!

And as I mused I saw around our sweet immortal sires,
Who kindled at the century's dawn fair freedom's vestal
    fires,   .
Bewailing for the perished hope of all their fond desires.

And in time's cycle, too, I saw, advance is all in vain,
Material triumps ever forced the moral back again,
Like tide extremes, which rise and fall equal upon the
    main.

And so I turned and left the spring that fair Nevada
    night;
The sun sank to as calm repose as though all things were
    bright;
And I as calmly thought, for God, " Whatever is, is right."

American Flat, July, 1876.

TWO LIVES.

To the Hon. A. A. S.—1874

Friend of the earnest, olden time,
'T was midst Nevada's hills of snow,
Near thirty fleeting years ago,
We met in manhood's early prime.

And I, though young, had roamed the earth,
My eyes had every country seen;
And borean region, tropic green,
Had seemed to claim me from my birth.

And *men* had bowed before my power,
My bark had sailed on every sea,
Proud in my strength, and bold as free,
I saw no tempests o'er me lower.

And yours? a slightly newer life,
Had all of fierce ambition's lure,
The power to *do*, and to endure,
And face the world in civic strife.

You chose the statesman's troubled path;
While I, as studiously inclined,
In abstract lore could only find
A shield from passion's storm of wrath.

I prayed that you might gain your end,
'T was music to my ears—the sound,
That you had gained another round
On fame's proud ladder, old time friend.

War came with tramp of marshaled foes;
Then from Mount Shasta's hoary head
To San Diego's coral bed,
One cry throughout our State arose:

" The man will be a Saviour true,
Who joins the homes and joins the hands
Of East to West in iron bands,
And brings the old time friends to view."

'T was yours within the halls of State
To introduce the high emprise,
To be the center of all eyes,
And be called greatest midst the great.

No triumph yet decreed by Rome,
For grand results in battle won,
For deeds of glory dared and done,
With greater honor welcomed home

Her Tribunes, than was then bestowed
On you, from all both high and low ;
Nor could be found a public foe
Amid their acclamations loud.

Time passed, a lurid light appears ;
Your image, once their idol God,
Was dragged in dust upon the sod,
And burned amid their jibes and jeers.

And you have seen that fame 's a sound:
Sometimes the mob would raise you high,
Then as of old shout " Crucify,"
And hunt their idol to the ground.

9

But then, when rained their curses fast,
Amid the execrations foul,
The base revilings of the crowd,
Some stood the same from first to last.

'T is well: I walk without a home,
Beneath the stars, a sentinel
Of felons in each darksome cell:
Your roof's the Capitolian dome.

I'm lost from home and place of birth;
But springing from my silent pen,
In many a vale, and dell, and glen,
Some flowers arise to bless the earth.

Against this power I count as dross
The treasures of the ancient Ind,
And all the diamonds slaves may find
Beneath the gleaming Southern Cross.

But you, in this material age,
No doubt did choose the better part;
The treasures of the hand, not heart,
You knew were best the war to wage

Against the fiends who cluster round
Your every path in public life;
Avarice and greed, and hate and strife—
Camp-followers on *your* battle-ground.

I pace my nigntly vigil long;
I wander hither, back and forth,
Like Cain, condemned to walk the earth,
Where only outcasts round me throng.

Above me shine the gleaming stars,
The same that omened ancient fates,
The fall of empires, thrones, and states,
Or threatened pestilence and wars.

I cannot hide me from their sight,
Their burning eyes look down on me;
They see my deep despondency,
And seem to know 't will end in *night.*

The law of compensation is,
The law of Nature always was,
The law that regulates all laws,
And guides the world's great harmonies.

I read the riddle thus: It seems
The waking hours to you are best,
By every dear surrounding blest;
I 'm only happy in my dreams.

Waking sometimes, it is the same,
I hear some grand old anthem roll:
It is the God within the soul,
And that is all the dower I claim.

We cannot tell, with all our lore,
Whether our forms this earth will grace
When to this very point in space
The earth has made one circuit more.

We cannot tell, with all our lore,
Of any good the spirit finds
In that which oft the spirit blinds—
I mean, excess of worldly store

Farewell, my friend: if I find one
True to his best convictions first,
Nor pleased to make the best the worst,
I 'll count not lost the race I 've run.

SAN QUENTIN, September, 1874

DAISY MORRIS.

I have builded me a cottage
  By the margin of the stream,
Where the golden sunlight lingers
  Till the day's departing beam.
All around my rustic cottage
  I have builded tiny bowers,
Waiting for my daisy darling
  To be queen among the flowers.

Round the porches and the windows
  Of this cottage home of mine
I have made the wild arbutus
  With the rhododendron twine.
There shall be no chilling winter
  In this cottage home of ours,
Only radiant, golden sunshine,
  Or refreshing, pearly showers.

Near my cottage, by the river,
　　Is a mountain, tall and steep;
At its base my kine are grazing,
　　On its sides are snow-white sheep.
On its crest are forest monarchs,
　　Giants of the olden time,
Never seen in any country
　　But our gorgeous western clime.

On some balmy summer morning
　　We will climb its summit high,
With our garden-home beneath us,
　　And above the azure sky.
And when evening shades are falling
　　And the setting sun declines,
You shall hear the vespers ringing
　　Through the branches of the pines.

I had roamed the wide world over,
　　Met the dark Italian's glance,
Seen the blondes of bonny England,
　　And the brown-eyed belles of France;
But my heart was cold as winter—
　　Never knew the thrill of love,
Till I met you, Daisy Morris—
　　You they call the " Mountain Dove."

Sometimes on the river's bosom
  In my boat we 'll gently glide:
There's no peril — I 'm a sailor,
  And know every change of tide.
I will row you where the branches
  O'er the limpid waters lean,
Adding loveliness enchanting
  To the beauty of the scene.

CHORUS

Can you love me, Daisy Morris?
  Will you come and dwell with me,
In my cottage near the river
  That is running to the sea?

NEW YEAR'S GREETING — 1879.

Passing years, like passing ages,
  Ever bring us something new;
And again, for History's pages,
  We the year's events review;
And rehearse, for retrospection,
  What of hope, or joy, or fear
Has been shadowed for our Nation
  During the departed.year.

First, despite of Old World troubles,
  Let the fact our hopes elate,
That among the growing nations
  We are greatest of the great!
Young in years, and young in feeling,
  Fresh from Nature, fresh from God,
We have gained a brighter future
  From beneath His chastening rod.

All that war and desolation
  Showered upon us in the past
Has procured a new salvation,
  Patriots swear, though time shall last.
Harvests gleam in bounteous plenty,
  No gaunt famine stalks the land;
Still we feed the Old World's millions
  With a free and lavish hand.

All the visions seen by prophets
  In the old and mighty East,
Find a more than full fruition
  In our new and wondrous West.
Gleams the harvest, weeps the vintage,
  Roam the flocks and sheds the fleece,
That were claimed for old Arcadia's
  Fabled realm of joy and peace.

When the pestilential demon
  Hovered round the flowery South
With delirium's frenzied fury
  And fell fever's deadly drouth;
From the Northland God's evangels
  Went, the sufferers' lot to share,
Though dread Azrael, death's dark angel,
  Hovered in the tainted air.

Open wide your eyes, ye scoffers!
    Who believe in regal chains!
Russia's eagle droops his feathers,
    While the Turkish crescent wanes.
Count ambition's fated victims,
    Sacrificed in bloody wars;
Count by thousands frozen faces,
    Upturned to the glimmering stars.

When their forces crossed the Balkans,
    When they fought on Plevna's height,
When the wolf and fierce hyena
    Feasted through the gloomy night;
When the pestilence went surging
    Through the starved battalions there,
To increase the broad dominions
    Of the grasping Northern Bear;

Then unto our star-gemmed banner,
    All exultant, cast your eyes;
While the unstained constellation
    Leads each glorious, grand emprize.
Now Columbia's genius speaking,
    Says to strife and tumult, "Cease!"
While from ocean unto ocean
    Spreads the olive branch of peace.

Stop, my muse!   One cloud of darkness
   Dims the present's burnished light,
Full of dark and gloomy portents,
   Moral pestilence, and blight;
Treatening in the hast'ning future
   Rapine, discord, blood, and spoil:
Alien slaves of alien masters
   Now degrade fair Freedom's soil.

There 's no danger that the people
   Will a century's work undo:
Danger comes from legislators,
   To their sacred trust untrue.
All should know that men or nations
   Who depart from thoughts refined,
Lured by base considerations,
   Shame the triumphs of the mind.

Not by idle, useless vaunting,
   Not by threat'nings vain and wild,
Not by sophistry or canting,
   Can be saved fair Freedom's child.
Not for base, ignoble trading,
   Shall our honor be laid low;
Shall they come?   The people's answer
   Must be one eternal No!

To more pleasing retrospection
  Of events, we now incline,
And Nevada claims some mention—
  Land of mountain, vale, and mine.
From where Carson's arbored city
  Sits amid oases green,
And Virginia, silver-sandaled,
  Stands the peerless Mountain Queen;

Here, where since the stars were singing
  At creation's early dawn,
And no sound disturbed the stillness,
  Save the Storm-King's shriek or moan;
Now the iron meteor gleaming
  Frights the wild beast from its lair,
While the Steam-King, fiercely screaming,
  Says: "Make way! my path prepare."

Poets sing of fair Italia—
  Land of beauty, mirth, and wine:
Progress gives us richer dowry
  Than the Old World can combine
Class the blessings that surronnd us,
  And to God your voices raise:
Never people on his footstool
  Had such cause to sing His praise.

www.ingramcontent.com/pod-product-compliance
Lightning Source LLC
Chambersburg PA
CBHW030542040726
47497CB00008B/2556